AMINATA COOTE

The Doctor's Christmas Miracle

First published by Hopelight Publishers 2024

Copyright © 2024 by Aminata Coote

Scripture quotations are from the King James Version of the Bible. Public domain.

Editor Latasha Strachan

Cover design by Hopelight Graphics

The Doctor's Christmas Miracle was first published in November 2023 as part of the anthology, A Merry Heart.

First edition

ISBN: 978 976 8334 19 0

This book was professionally typeset on Reedsy.
Find out more at reedsy.com

Contents

One

Meeting Doctor Grump

Optimism was a choice—one Elena Fairchild made several times a day. Of course, having the nickname of Sunshine made cheerfulness almost a requirement.

She made that choice as the bus drove past the Welcome to Orange Valley sign. She would be the best maid of honor ever. Even if she was a little jealous that her 54-year-old mother was getting married for the second time, while her dating prospects remained nonexistent.

She was the only passenger to disembark, not surprising since most people drove themselves these days. Sunshine grabbed her hard-shell suitcase from the luggage bay and blew out a breath.

Her mother was supposed to pick her up from the terminal, but with Trixie, she could be anywhere from a few minutes to several hours late.

Sunshine dug her cell phone from her backpack and called her mother.

Trixie was flustered when she answered. "Hi, sweetie. How are you?"

"Cold." Orange Valley was at least ten degrees cooler than Portsville. "I'm at the terminal waiting for you to pick me up."

"Was that today?"

Sunshine did a quick count to ten in her head. "Yes, Mom, December 14, two weeks before your wedding, as you requested."

Sunshine had saved her vacation time and almost started the third world war when she'd requested time off during the busiest wedding season of the year.

Only the fact that she'd gotten people to cover her flower jobs had made it possible for her to be in Orange Valley.

"Oh, Sunny, I'm sorry. I can't pick you up. I'm in Idlewood."

Cheerfulness was a choice. Sunshine imagined herself in a field of sunflowers and focused on keeping calm.

"Why are you in Idlewood, Mom?"

"Oh, it was the funniest thing. I had a dream last night that I should have a cake made out of cupcakes, so I drove up to Idlewood to ask Regina if she could bake three hundred cupcakes for my wedding."

"Three hundred—?" Sunshine pulled out the handle of her suitcase and headed toward the exit. "Do you know how long it would take for her to bake that many cupcakes? Especially since she's running a bakery."

Gina's Bakery was one of the most famous pastry shops on Saturn Island. It was not uncommon for people to drive miles to get one of Regina's creations.

"Regina said the same thing," Trixie's tone was sulky.

Sunshine speed-walked to the taxi stand.

"Mom, we talked about this."

"What do you mean, Sunny?"

Sunshine lifted an arm to grab the attention of the hackney cab.

"You will not be a bridezilla."

"Keith doesn't think I'm Bridezilla."

"That's because Keith believes you invented sliced bread."

Keith West was the sweetest man Sunshine had ever met. He treated her mother like a queen—something Trixie deserved after losing her husband at such a young age.

"I have to go, Mom. I'll call you when I get to the house."

Sunshine hefted her suitcase into the trunk and slid into the back seat, slamming the door behind her.

The driver glared at her in the rearview mirror.

"Sorry. It got away from me." Just as her temper had almost gotten away from her.

"A merry heart does good, like medicine, but a broken spirit dries the bones."

"What was that, dear?" The elderly woman sitting beside her turned in Sunshine's direction.

"Nothing," She dredged up a smile. "I was reminding myself to enjoy this beautiful day. I have a lot to be thankful for."

"That's a nice attitude to have, dear. I wish more people saw things your way."

Sunshine angled her body toward the older woman. She loved talking to people from other generations. She learned so much.

She enjoyed talking to people, period. It was one reason she was the most sought-after florist in Portsville. Her ability to connect with people made it easier to get them to explain their vision to her. The more she understood what they envisioned for their wedding, the easier her job became.

Creating the perfect floral arrangement for her clients used to bring her joy, but now it gave her a massive headache. Not that she'd ever admit it to anyone.

Sunshine smiled at the older woman. "Have you always lived in Orange Valley?"

By the time the car stopped in front of her mother's house, Sunshine had learned the woman was having a hip replacement the next day and had made plans to visit her in the hospital.

She waved to Daisy and the cab driver, Tim, before dragging her suitcase up the short flight of stairs to her mother's veranda.

Her chest warmed as she admired the potted plants that her mom had decorated for Christmas. Each had a unique design, but the bright red against the green reminded Sunshine how much she loved the colors of Christmas.

The only thing missing was the red and black checkered cushion covers that should have replaced the more serviceable year-round ones. Those and the matching blanket they usually threw over the back of the patio chair, so it was available if someone wanted to sit on the veranda without freezing. She'd get it out of storage and finish up the decorating for her mom.

Thankful that she had keys to the house, Sunshine let herself in. She drew in a huge breath of cinnamon spice with a hint of peppermint and grinned. Her mother's signature scent brought childhood memories flooding back.

Christmas had always been family time, at least it had been until she'd moved away. Sunshine shook off the lingering thoughts of work. This was her vacation, and she intended to soak up as much Christmassy goodness as possible.

Her mother had set up the Christmas tree and pulled out the

decorations, but hadn't decorated it. Sunshine grinned. She loved Christmas. It was single-handedly the best holiday of the year.

This was the first Christmas in a long time that she wouldn't be busy designing floral arrangements for someone else's happily ever after. Of course, that wasn't quite right either, since she'd be doing the flowers for her mother's wedding.

She called her mom again. "Please tell me you got me something off Regina's Christmas menu."

Every year, Regina had an exclusive selection only available from December through the first week of January. She changed the menu often, though there were some things, such as her sorrel cookies that remained staples.

Trixie giggled. "Of course I did."

"Good. We can eat them while we set this tree up."

"Oh, sweetie, I can't help you set things up today. Keith's taking me out to dinner."

On her first night back in town? Things were already changing, and not for the better, as far as Sunshine was concerned.

She took a deep breath. It wasn't Keith's fault, since Trixie had forgotten she was coming today.

Besides, she didn't need her mother to entertain her. She'd be perfectly fine setting things up on her own.

"That's okay, Mom. You and Keith have fun."

She disconnected and dropped the phone on the couch. She could do this all by herself. Sunshine cracked her knuckles.

"Alright, Sunshine, let's decorate this tree." She pulled up her playlist of nineties Christmas songs and got to work.

* * *

Matthew Beckett hated Christmas and everything associated with it. He hated the artificial cheerfulness and the music playing constantly on the overhead stereos. As if anyone would forget they were ill because of a few songs talking about Santa Claus or Jesus.

And why were the colors of this holiday so bright? It was as if whoever had created Christmas wanted to force everyone to adopt his false cheer.

"Doctor Beckett," the head nurse waved to him as he stomped past the nurses' station. "You have a minute?"

She had the phone cradled between her shoulder and ear as she rummaged for something on the desk.

If someone hadn't stuck a potted cacti plant overladen with garlands on the desk, she wouldn't have trouble finding whatever she was looking for.

"Is this going to take all day, Nurse Richards?" He scowled at her.

He had at least two patients to visit before tonight's dinner with his grandfather. The only excuse for missing one of those was a severe medical emergency or someone's death. Preferably his.

"Let me call you back after I'm done dealing with GD." She slammed the phone into the cradle.

GD—Grumpy Doctor or Grinchy Doctor depending on the time of year. Matt was aware that most of the staff disliked him, but he wasn't at Morningside to win popularity contests.

He was there to help his patients, and if he saved someone's life, all the better. His patients didn't need him to be Doctor Congeniality. They needed his expertise.

"You wanted to know when the patient in Room 608 was awake. She woke up half an hour ago."

And he was just being told? He arched his brows but didn't say a word.

"We paged you, but there was no response."

He gave a brusque nod. "I'll check on her."

He pivoted toward the direction he'd been coming from. If he spent seven point five minutes with Daisy Dane and drove two miles per hour faster, he'd get to his grandfather's with two minutes to spare and avoid a lecture.

Matt increased his speed slightly to improve the odds in his favor. If he moved fast enough, he'd have another thirty seconds to spend with his patient.

Matt entered Daisy Dane's room and blinked. "What is going on here?"

Every available surface had a vase with flowers. A large helium balloon with the words "Get Well Soon" floated on the ceiling.

"Isn't it great?" A woman in a mustard sweater and jeans beamed at him.

"No, it is not great," he scowled at her. "You've turned this hospital room into a garden."

She grinned. "That was kind of the point. A cheerful environment helps a patient's recovery."

"Oh?" He gave her his full attention. "Are you a doctor, Miss...?"

She laughed, the sound reminiscent of the detested silver bells he'd been hearing all season.

"No, I'm not a doctor. I'm a florist."

"Figured."

Matt let out a tiny breath of relief and hurried to his patient's bedside. The idea that Ms. Dane had brought in a consultant had grated at him.

He scanned the elderly woman lying flat in the bed, noting her pallor and checking the monitors beside her.

"How are you feeling?"

Ms. Dane gave him a baleful look. "Like someone cut me open and poked around in my hip."

Matt sensed the presence by his shoulder before the woman spoke.

"Can't you give her something for the pain?"

"Is she your daughter, Ms. Dane?"

"No." The woman smiled slowly. "This is Sunshine. I met her yesterday in the cab and told her I was having surgery and she offered to visit."

There were so many things wrong with her statement that Matt wasn't sure where to start.

He snorted. "Your name is Sunshine?"

"Yes." She moved around to the other side of the hospital bed and glared at him. "What's it to you?"

"Nothing." Matt shook his head. "I'm always curious about parents who saddle their children with names that belong in the dictionary."

She rolled her eyes. "I suppose you have an ostentatious name, like Augustine or Bryce."

Why were they having this ridiculous conversation?

"Why are you still here?" He glared and pointed to the door. "Out."

"Well," she huffed out a breath. "I'm not going to stay here and be insulted by this-this grump!" She leaned down and gave Ms. Dane a sweet smile. "I'll come back after the Grouch leaves."

She thrust back her shoulders and did a remarkable job of strutting out of Daisy Dane's room.

Two

A Frosty Alliance

Sunshine stalked out of Daisy's room. What a horrible man! If he hadn't seemed genuinely concerned about Daisy, she'd have been worried about leaving Doctor Grumpy in the room with her.

She spun in a circle. What was she supposed to do while he was checking on her new friend? It was visiting hour, so most people had family and friends spending time with them.

Daisy's forlorn face from the previous day flashed in her mind. Maybe not. She wandered the hall, checking for rooms not overrun with visitors. Halfway down the corridor, she found one.

She stuck her head into the room where an old man sat in a hospital bed, a bandage around his eyes.

"Hello?" His voice boomed across the space. "Who is it? Nurse? Doctor?"

What if that grumpy doctor ran her out of this room too?

"Please." The man's voice was plaintive. "Would you talk to me, please?"

Sunshine stepped into the room. The poor man was practically begging her to speak with him. What was the harm? She may as well keep his company.

Sunshine cleared her throat. "Hi."

The man angled his head in her direction. "You sound pretty."

She grinned, drawing nearer to the bed. "I bet you were a heartbreaker when you were young."

The man's lips curled into a kind smile. "I never broke a woman's heart, Miss. I took great care of it until she wanted it back." He stuck a hand in her general direction. "The name's Gerald."

"Hi, Gerald." She took his wrinkled hand in hers. "I'm Sunshine."

"You wouldn't have a few minutes to spend with a lonely old man, would you?"

She checked her watch. In less than fifteen minutes, the visiting hour would be over and she'd have to leave. But there was no way she was going back to Daisy's room until she was sure the cantankerous old doctor was gone.

Okay, so he wasn't old. He couldn't have been more than a couple of years older than her. His green eyes were the exact shade of her favorite Christmas ornament, and that firm jaw made her wish—

She snapped her thought in the middle. She wouldn't wish for anything. She was not in Orange Valley to find a date. And if she had been, it wouldn't be a snappy doctor who thought too much of himself.

"I can sit for a few minutes." She plopped into the chair beside his bed. "Where's your family?" Nobody should have to be in the hospital alone—especially not at Christmas.

"My daughter and her husband were supposed to be here. They're flying in from the States, but their flight was grounded because of a storm."

"Oh," Sunshine whispered a prayer for their safety. "So, Gerald, why are you spending your holiday in the hospital?"

"You again?"

Sunshine's head snapped up at the familiar, disgruntled voice. She stifled a groan.

Why is this man stalking me, Lord?

"Don't you have anything better to do than follow me around?"

He folded his arms across his chest—his impressive arms. Surely he didn't get those muscles from his daily activities?

"Unlike you, I have a reason to be here." He pointed to the badge clipped to his lab coat as he moved closer to the bed.

"Once again, you're impeding my ability to do my job." He thrust a thumb over his shoulder.

"Yeah, yeah." She pushed to her feet. "I'll check on you tomorrow, Gerald, if you're still here."

On impulse, she leaned over and kissed his grizzled cheek. She angled her head as she brushed past the doctor, his spicy clove scent wafting to her nose. Why did such a bad-tempered man smell so good?

And she had no business sniffing Doctor Grouch or anything to do with him. She ducked back into Daisy's room, but her friend was already asleep. Good. Hopefully, he'd given her something for the pain.

Sunshine lay a gentle hand on Daisy's arm. "Father, I commit Daisy into Your care. I pray that You will heal her and keep her safe. Amen."

God would take care of her friend. She had an inkling to pray for the grumpy doctor, but she brushed it off. Nah. He already occupied too much room in her head. It was time to think about something else. Preferably something cheerful, like what she'd be having for dinner that night or her mother's wedding.

On her way out of the room, she bumped into a nurse's aide and sent the papers in the woman's hand flying.

"Oh, I'm sorry." Sunshine dropped to the ground and scooped up a handful of papers, stashing them together.

"It's okay." The young woman laughed, her elf hat tipped at a daring angle. "I know better than to walk so close to the doors. The first week I worked here, I was always bumping into someone."

They both stood, and Sunshine handed the papers she'd collected to the woman.

"Thanks." The aide looked her up and down. "You wouldn't be interested in helping with our fundraiser, would you?"

She should say no. This was supposed to be a vacation—the only break she'd have for at least six months. One that she'd be spending to design the floral arrangements for her mother's wedding.

"It would only take a couple of hours of effort." The woman clapped her hands together and pouted her lips while making puppy dog eyes at Sunshine.

She chuckled. "If you're going to be manipulating me this early in our relationship, I should at least know your name."

The young woman laughed and stuck out her hand. "I'm Zoë."

"Nice to meet you, Zoë." She grasped the woman's hand. "My name's Sunshine."

Zoë's face lit up. "I love that."

She flashed a grin of thanks. "What's this thing you're trying to get me to sign up for?"

Zoë handed her a typewritten sheet of paper. Sunshine scanned the piece of paper but learned no more information than Zoë had provided.

"This doesn't provide a lot of details."

Zoë groaned. "I know. The trouble is we want to have this fundraiser, but we don't have a clue what we're doing yet."

Sunshine's eyes widened. "But there's a date on here."

Zoë's head bobbed up and down, and there was a sheen of desperation in her eyes. "Will you help?"

Sunshine gulped. Ten years of serving frantic brides made this more of an adventure and less of a challenge. She'd work it in around everything else.

"Count me in."

* * *

Matt slunk into the staff meeting a few minutes after it started. His patient consultation took longer than expected. And yes, while he always loved being on a schedule, something about Shantoy got to him.

The teenager had persevered against all the odds stacked against her. She'd pushed past the limitations of her scoliosis diagnosis, risen to the top of her class, and, remained active in school activities and her community.

He leaned against the wall as far away from the rest of the staff as possible. Not that he had any success because, as usual, the room was too small for the staff meeting and didn't have enough seating.

He checked the agenda on his phone. What had he missed? Oh, good, only the insincere appreciation offered by the head of the department.

The man stood at the front of the room, his bald head glistening with sweat. Probably because the air-conditioning was struggling to cool the room with so many people in it.

Or because there was too much wool stuffed into this room since everyone somehow managed to include either gaudy pants or a tacky sweater in their outfit. A ridiculous decision because the temperature in the hospital was the same as it would have been at any other time of year.

"I called this meeting because we have yet to decide on the fundraiser we're hosting in two weeks."

Matt scowled. This was about a fundraiser? Not an effective use of his time. Not when he had patients who needed his help. He sidled to his left, keeping his eyes fixed on Jack Turner, not wanting to draw any attention to himself.

"Need I remind you this fundraiser will assist some of our patients—the ones struggling to pay their medical bills?"

Matt jerked to a halt. The fundraiser was for medical aid.

"Dr. Beckett. Are you volunteering?"

As a unit, everyone swung to stare at him.

"Uh, no." He pointed to the exit. "I was..."

"Sneaking out of the meeting?"

His face went hot as snickers filled the room.

"I don't have time to show up at a bunch of meetings. There's a hospital full of sick people."

Turner sighed. "I know you consider these meetings to not be worth your time."

He and Turner had never seen eye to eye, ever since they'd started working at Morningside Hospital within six months of each other. Turner was all process, whereas Matt disliked the way paperwork sometimes hampered him from helping the people who needed him.

Matt buttoned his lips. Experience had taught him that answering Turner wouldn't work in his favor.

"Extending yourself to participate in programs put on by the hospital is expected by every member of this team. This will be a consideration when the hospital goes to renew a doctor's contract."

Matt narrowed his eyes at the man. Was this a lecture? He'd lost track of the number of meetings he'd endured because someone had complained about his lack of participation. He didn't care what these people did after working hours, and he had no desire to spend any more time with them than was necessary.

There was also a hint of a threat in Turner's statement. Was the man suggesting that Morningside wouldn't renew his contract because he didn't play nice with the other residents? How real was that threat?

Matt was coming up on his three-year anniversary in a few months. Would he need to start job hunting?

Turner sighed and swiped a palm over his shiny pate. "I thought you'd have been interested in signing up since some of the proceeds are supposed to go towards one of your patient's surgery."

His eyebrows shot up. Most of his patients had insurance except—

"Which patient?"

Turner's eyes dipped to the tablet in front of him. "Shantoy Ducasse."

Matt's heart sank like a stone. That young girl, with her

whole life ahead of her, depended on this hospital being able to raise the funds for her surgery?

He growled. "When's the first meeting?"

By the time Matt slipped into the tiny conference room that had been reserved for the meeting, he was already regretting his decision to help. Especially since he was the only person there. After all his talk about holiday spirit, Matt had expected Turner to be the first person in the room.

He sucked his teeth and spun to leave. This was a waste of his time.

He collided with something soft and warm and barely had the presence of mind to hold on firmly.

"Thanks." A tinkling laugh assaulted his ears. "Those doorways are lethal."

Matt thrust the floral-scented woman away from him and scowled.

"Do you always smell like a bouquet?"

She arched a symmetrical brow. "Would you prefer if I smelled like a pharmacy?"

She stomped to the small conference table, plunked down a backpack, and began dragging things out of it.

"What are you doing here?"

She smirked at him. "Must be a slow day for you. Don't you have any patients to terrorize?"

Matt folded his arms across his chest and glowered. He wasn't proud of it, but his scowl had caused more than one intern to burst into tears.

She plunked a tin of cookies into the center of the table and ignored him. Was he losing his touch?

The door flew inward, and another woman whirled in. Didn't these women walk? He glared at the newcomer, an aide with an improbable letter name. Yasmin? Winifred?

"Hey, Zoë." Sunshine greeted the other woman with a bright smile. "Where's everyone else?"

"This is it, I'm afraid." Zoë gave an apologetic smile. "Although Paul from Pediatrics said I should tell him if there's anything he can help with."

Sunshine's gaze flitted from Zoë to him. "I guess working in the hospital means you guys believe in miracles."

He snorted. Why wasn't he surprised she believed in impossible things?

She turned to him, her hands propped on her waist. "Don't tell me, Doctor Grouch, that you don't believe in miracles."

"Miracles are nothing more than coincidences given more importance because of an overactive imagination."

Sunshine's mouth dropped open. Had he silenced the woman? It was about time. If the sudden quiet made him uncomfortable, it was only because he was conscious of the minutes ticking away while he did nothing.

He turned his glare on Zoë. "I take it she's here to help plan the fundraiser?"

Zoë nodded, her eyes huge, as if she would burst out crying any second. Oh, for pity's sake. Why did these people apply for jobs in a hospital if they teared up at the slightest provocation? He waved his hand.

"Well, go on then. Start the meeting."

He hadn't believed it possible, but Zoë's eyes widened further.

"Oh, no. I know nothing about putting on a fundraiser. The only reason I'm here is because I'm familiar with using the copy machine."

Matt swiped a hand over his face. Great. They'd be there all day. Three people who wanted to be somewhere else.

"I—" Zoë thrust some papers at him. "Why don't you do it?"

"Me?" He gaped at the woman. What, in her interaction with him, gave her the impression he had any idea how to plan a fundraiser? If Turner hadn't called him out in front of everyone, he wouldn't be here.

The reason he was still here was because he wanted Shantoy to have her surgery. He stared at the papers Zoë was practically crushing against his chest, but refused to move a muscle.

"You two are ridiculous." Sunshine snatched the papers from Zoë's hand, the back of her hand grazing his chest. Heat burned through him as if she'd sliced him with a scalpel.

"You sit there." She jabbed a finger toward him, then at a chair. "You over there." She pointed to a chair on the opposite side, waiting until he and Zoë sat.

She stood at the head of the table and glared at him. Since he was recovering from whatever had happened when she'd touched him, he simply stared back, trying to regain his composure.

"It's obvious if we leave this up to any of you guys, we'll be here until the end of time. I'll do it."

Matt opened his mouth to protest, though he had no idea why. He didn't want the job.

"What qualifies you to plan a fundraiser?"

She narrowed her eyes at him. "I do flowers for one of the most sought-after wedding planners in Portsville. This can't be harder than planning a wedding. Of course, Doctor," she said his title like a curse. "I'm sure with your superior knowledge and experience, we'll have this event planned in no time. Why don't you take over?"

What? How did they get back here? He raised his palms in surrender, conceding.

"Why don't you give it a shot first? At this point, we have nothing to lose."

And maybe by the time things got critical, Turner would round up a few more volunteers.

Three

Electric Encounters

Sunshine pushed open the door of The Fair Child. "Mom? I've got food."

After the near-disastrous meeting at the hospital, she'd stopped at a fast-food restaurant and bought chicken and chips.

"Where are you?"

Sunshine took a second to appreciate the flower shop her father had opened before she'd been born. It was like stepping into a garden. The shop floor had several small tables laden with flowers—mostly potted plants that sold fairly quickly. Blooms of every color filled the three-door floral cooler.

The counter where her mother normally worked had a selection of flowers and a partially filled vase.

Her mother bustled in from the office, her hair mussed. Trixie Fairchild was a pretty woman. Her black hair, which she wore in a short bob, had only a few streaks of silver.

"Mom?" Sunshine narrowed her eyes. "What were you doing?"

"Nothing." Trixie brushed a hand over her hair, angling her body between Sunshine and the half-open office door. "I was checking the books."

"Right." Her mother hated accounting more than she hated the sight of dirty dishes. It was the reason Sunshine had done the books in high school, and why she'd insisted they hire a bookkeeper before she'd left for Portsville to intern at Bella Flora.

She dredged up a bright smile for her mom. "Let's eat." She handed her mother the bag with their lunch and the drink carrier. "Why don't you take these? I need to wash my hands."

Trixie grabbed the food, and Sunshine used her mother's distraction to dash past her into the office. She flicked on the light and jerked to a halt at the sheepish expression of her mother's fiance.

"Keith?" She ran her gaze over the man's disheveled appearance. "What are you doing in here?" Alone. In the dark.

"Sunshine! You tricked me." Trixie's wail came from behind her.

Keith avoided her gaze and tugged on his tie—his slightly crooked tie. Her eyes ran between Keith and Trixie. Wait.

Sunshine gaped at her mother. "Were you guys in here making out?"

Trixie sniffed and brushed past Sunshine. "I'll have you know, Sunshine," she linked arms with Keith, "I'm a grown woman and an engaged one at that." She leaned over and pecked Keith on the cheek.

"Oh, please." Sunshine clapped a hand over her eyes. "Make it stop."

Her mother giggled. "If you'd stop pushing people away, you'd find your own guy."

Sunshine snorted. "I don't push people away. I'm always cheerful and upbeat."

Trixie's gaze filled with compassion. "Barriers come in all shapes and sizes, Elena. Sometimes, you use cheerfulness as a shield."

What a ridiculous notion. She didn't use cheerfulness as a shield. Her mother was doing what people in love did—hinting that Sunshine was missing out on something because she was single.

"Yes, well," Sunshine said as she backed out of the office. "I'm going to disinfect my eyes after this display." She flipped the switch.

"Wait." Her mother's cry stopped her in her tracks. "Keith and I have something to say to you. Would you turn on the light?" Trixie's voice was disgruntled.

"Sorry," Sunshine snickered. "I was giving you space to go back to what you were doing before—while protecting my eyes."

"Ha-ha." Trixie slid her hand down to link with Keith's.

Sunshine suppressed a sigh. She wanted that. Someone who loved her because of who she was. Someone to lean on. Why was it that God hadn't seen it fit to send her the perfect guy?

For everything there is a season.

"What did you want to talk to me about?" She adopted a pleasant expression.

Jealousy did nothing but eat out a person's inside. And envying her mom was just wrong. The woman had sacrificed a lot for Sunshine, especially after her father's death.

"Well," Keith smiled at Sunshine. "It's more of an invitation.

We're having dinner with my son and his wife this evening and want you to join us."

"Sure." She smiled at the man who would be her stepfather in a couple of weeks. She'd missed most of his courtship of her mother because she lived so far away. This would be a chance to make sure he was as nice as he seemed.

"Wear something pretty." Trixie beamed at her.

"Why?"

Keith massaged the back of his neck. "Ian will probably invite his best friend to join us."

She smothered a groan. She hated blind dates. It would be uncomfortable enough to meet her future in-laws without the added pressure of an unwanted date.

"Sunshine." Her mother's eyes bore into hers. "Be nice." Trixie mouthed the words. Sunshine plastered on a fake smile.

"Keith and I are going to finish up here, and then I want to talk flowers."

Finally. That was one of the main reasons she'd come to Orange Valley after all.

"Sure, Mom, I'll order a bell for the front door so you can hear when I come into the store."

Trixie made a face. "You're a comedian."

Sunshine grinned. "In the meantime, you kids don't do anything I wouldn't do." She pulled the door closed behind her.

Later that evening, Sunshine slid her hands down the front of her yellow cocktail dress.

"You look lovely." Trixie pressed her face close to Sunshine's, and the scent of lavender wafted around them. "It's unconventional for a woman my age to be getting married, but I believe it's the right thing to do."

Sunshine turned to face her mom. Had she made her mother question her decision to marry Keith?

"Does he make you happy?"

Trixie nodded. "Yes. He reminds me of your father in some ways."

Sunshine swallowed. Her father had died when she was five, so her memories of him were hazy. But her mom talked about him all the time. Sunshine grew up knowing her parents had loved each other.

"Okay. Then you don't need my approval."

Trixie grabbed her hand. "I want it."

Sunshine nodded. Her first impulse was to tell her mother she approved of Keith, but she held back. Because she couldn't give her one hundred percent approval. Not yet.

"I'll spend some time with him before the wedding." So that when she gave her approval, it would be genuine.

"That's all I ask," Trixie squeezed her arm. "Now, let's go meet your new brother. You'll like Ian, and Marie is a sweetheart."

She hoped, no, she *would* like them. These people were important to Trixie, and she'd do her best to welcome them into the family.

* * *

Matt climbed out of his car and scowled at his best friends. "Why'd I agree to this again?"

They'd met in a first-year English course at university after being thrust into a group together, and been friends ever since. Ian and Marie had married a year after graduation and shared an office where they specialized in marriage counseling.

Ian clapped him on the shoulder. "Because underneath that

bulldog exterior, you're a nice guy."

His scowl deepened. "Why do you assume your future step-sister will appreciate your attempts to even out the numbers?"

He should be at home, watching football. But he'd lost a bet, and this was the payment Ian had demanded.

"You'll be fine." Marie shifted to stand between him and Ian. It was what she'd always done. "I'm sure she'll appreciate not being the fifth wheel."

He huffed out a breath. "Let's get this over with."

"Look at it this way," Ian grinned at him. "You get a free meal out of it."

True. One less meal he had to prepare for himself.

He remained a few steps behind his friends as they entered the restaurant. At least this one didn't pipe Christmas music through the overhead speakers.

"There's Dad." Ian pointed to a table in the center of the room.

Keith's fiancee was an attractive woman with short hair. A flash of color caught his attention at the same time Marie gasped.

"I love the color of her dress."

Matt jerked to a stop. "No. I'm not doing this." He'd have stomped out of the restaurant if not for Ian's grip on his arm.

"What are you doing, man?"

Several diners gawked at them. Matt turned the full force of his scowl on them until only the most blatant ones kept staring.

"Ian." Keith West waved at them.

Matt huffed. Too late now. He followed his friends to the table and hung back during the introductions.

"You're Ian's friend?" The older woman, Trixie—where did these people get their names?—beamed at him.

"This is the Grump Who Hates Christmas, Mom," Sunshine smirked at him and Matt had the unexpected desire to grin.

Trixie's head volleyed between him and her daughter.

"The Grump—"

He extended a hand. "My parents named me Matthew Beckett, but friends call me Matt." He gave Sunshine a baleful glance. "Only women who believe they're Santa's helpers call me The Grump."

Ian's shoulders shook with silent laughter, but Matt ignored him. "Shall we sit?"

Ian and Marie claimed the seats near Trixie and Keith, leaving the one closer to Sunshine for him. Great.

A server came to take their orders, and Matt used the distraction as an opportunity to gather his thoughts. When he'd agreed to accompany Ian to his "meet the new family dinner", he'd been focused on fulfilling the terms of the bet he'd lost. The free meal had been a secondary consideration. What were the odds that Ian's future stepsister was Sunshine?

The second the server left with their orders, Trixie drew Ian into a conversation.

"So," Sunshine leaned closer to him. "Why are you stalking me?"

He snorted. Partly to dissuade her erroneous belief and partly to dispel the smell of flowers that always surrounded her. Did she sleep in a garden? Or was it some secret scent that emanated from her skin? Matt shook his head to dispel the fanciful thought. This woman was wrecking his equilibrium.

"Please," he met her gaze. For a second, he lost himself in the caramel-colored depths.

What were they talking about?

"Did you hear what I said, Matt?" Marie's voice brimmed

with amusement.

"No. Sorry." He'd been too busy staring into Sunshine's eyes like a lovesick fool. The tips of his ears burned.

"She was asking how you and Sunshine met," Ian repeated his wife's question, his eyes filled with amusement.

"He's stalking me."

"She's stalking me."

He and Sunshine spoke at the same time.

"Come again?" Keith frowned at them. "Is that a joke?" As a retired police officer, Keith took stalking seriously.

Matt sighed. "Yes, sir. Sunshine and I keep bumping into each other."

"Only because you keep showing up places where I'm at," Sunshine muttered the words under her breath.

"Oh?" Trixie's face lit up. "I've found that when that happens, it means God has a special plan in place."

"Oh, I don't believe in God."

Everything happened in slow motion. Trixie's mouth dropped open. Ian and Marie stared at him in exasperation. Keith's face flooded with disappointment, and Sunshine jerked her head to gawk at him.

Heat flooded his face, and for a second, he wished he had as much melanin in his skin as the others at the table.

"Figured." Sunshine rolled her eyes. "No wonder you're in such a bad mood all the time."

"I'm in a bad mood because I don't believe in your God?" His brow furrowed as he struggled to follow her logic. Were all women this confusing, or just her?

His eyes shifted to Marie before flickering back to Sunshine. He'd never had trouble understanding Marie, which meant the fault lay with Sunshine.

"No." She pressed her lips together. "You're grumpy because you believe this whole thing," she twirled her finger in a circle, "revolves around you."

Matt opened his mouth to protest. He was tired of people assuming every doctor had a god complex.

"I'm not finished." Sunshine jabbed a finger in his direction. "You're grumpy, Doctor Crabby, because you can't see how you fit into the bigger picture."

Her eyes were alight with passion. "God created this big beautiful world for us and gave you the skills and gifts to glorify His name, and you deny Him—"

"You call your beliefs faith," he butted in. "I call them delusions."

Sunshine snorted. "*I'm* deluded? You turn your back on the Creator and give credit for His marvelous creation to a ball of gas. Which one of us has the greater faith? The one who believes in an eternal Creator God? Or the one who believed gas appeared out of nowhere and swirled until there was a gigantic explosion that created everything in our universe?"

Matt snapped his mouth shut. He'd been challenged for his lack of belief before, but never before had he felt so…small. Her explanation of the Big Bang Theory was a little simplistic, but what if she was right? Did it take more faith to believe in the Big Bang than in her God?

Four

Bah, Humbug

The next morning, Sunshine was still seething over Matt's comment. How could he not believe in God? She slammed a saucepan with water onto the stove and lit the burner.

She wasn't naive—she knew some people didn't believe in God. She'd met people who were at different points in their faith journey than she was. But for someone to so blatantly disregard the existence of the Creator? Unbelievable.

She took out her anger on the green plantains, slicing them with more speed than skill.

"Are you orchestrating a visit to the hospital?"

Sunshine jumped at her mother's voice. "What are you talking about?"

Trixie gestured to the knife. "If you keep going at that speed, you'll hurt yourself. Of course, if it meant a visit to Doctor Matt, I'd take a chance." Trixie tittered.

Sunshine stopped chopping to stare at her mom. "Did you hear what he said last night? He doesn't believe in God, Mom. I can't be with somebody like that."

"I'm not suggesting you marry him, Sunshine. But since the two of you have to work together, try not to flay him with your tongue."

Oh, but she wanted to. Doctor Killjoy needed to find out how wrong he was not to believe in God.

"I don't get it, Mom." Sunshine resumed her slicing at a safer pace. "After studying the human body and seeing how intricately everything's connected, how each part affects the other, how could he not be a believer?"

She slid the sliced plantains into the blender with coconut milk and a pinch of salt. Trixie rested a hand on her arm.

"Did it occur to you that this is God reaching out to Matt through you? Use your words and actions to show Matt why you believe." Trixie shrugged. "Maybe he has a reason for not believing."

Sunshine opened her mouth to protest.

"Or," Trixie continued, one brow arched. "He's been hurt and is speaking from a place of pain. You won't know which it is unless you take the time to find out."

Trixie gave her a baleful look. "Pushing him away by preaching doctrine won't change his mind." Her mother stepped away to pull vanilla and spices out of the cupboard. "You can win more battles with kindness than by being antagonistic."

Sunshine pureed the ingredients in the blender. Was her mother right? Would she be a more effective witness for God by being nice than by keeping Matthew Beckett at a distance?

God, what do I do? I want to defend Your name. How do I do that?

Pleasant words are as an honeycomb, sweet to the soul, and health to the bones.

Sunshine poured the smooth mixture into the boiling water. She stirred to blend everything.

"There's a proverb for that." Trixie smiled at her.

She and her mother had been playing the Proverbs game for years after her mother claimed the Bible had an answer for everything. Sunshine had found the pithy sayings in the book of Proverbs easy to memorize while offering bite-sized advice.

She'd memorized most of the book, along with countless other verses that had encouraged her faith.

"Oh?" She arched a brow at her mom.

"A soft answer turneth away wrath: but grievous words stir up anger," Trixie recited.

"Good one." Sunshine agreed, "But the one I had in mind was, 'The tongue of the wise useth knowledge aright: but the mouth of fools poureth out foolishness.'" She angled her chin.

"Doctor Glum is the fool who denies the presence of God, but I will be the wise woman speaking truth and light in his life."

"When pride cometh, then cometh shame: but with the lowly is wisdom." Trixie smiled gently at her. "Don't let your pride lead you down the wrong path."

Sunshine nodded to acknowledge her mom's words. It was advice that she intended to heed, just as she planned to smother Matt's grumpiness with kindness. Let's see if he still doubted God's existence when she was done with him.

After breakfast, Trixie volunteered to wash dishes.

"Oh, good," Sunshine smiled at her mom, "because I'm leaving now."

"Where are you going?" Trixie's voice pitched up. "Aren't

you helping me in the flower shop?"

Sunshine tilted her head. "Was I supposed to?"

She ran through her memory for any conversation they may have had about it.

Trixie's hands fluttered. "I thought you'd assist in the shop for a couple of hours the way you normally do."

"I'm planning the hospital fundraiser." Hadn't they just talked about that?

"But I need your help at the shop." Trixie mock-pouted. "I have wedding things."

Still? Her mom was getting married in less than two weeks. Shouldn't most of the things have already been taken care of? Then again, she was still waiting for Trixie to tell her what kind of flowers she wanted for her wedding.

The only reason Sunshine wasn't freaking out was because she had an idea of what she wanted to create for her mom and had access to a ready supply of flowers.

"Oh-kay," Sunshine mentally recalculated all she had to do. "Why don't I take care of the shop in the evenings while you work the morning shift?"

That should give her enough time to put things in motion for the hospital fundraiser.

"Fine." Trixie waved a hand. "But we may have to change things around if I have a conflict."

"That works—please tell me in advance." Sunshine snuck a look at her mom. Trixie was acting weird. Was it wedding stress or something else?

* * *

Matt tapped the steering wheel as he waited for the light to change. This fundraiser thing was taking more time than he wanted to give. If not for his genuine desire to help Shantoy and the other patients, he'd have backed out.

He pulled into a parking spot in front of the parish council building as someone on a bicycle zipped in beside him.

Which idiot would ride a bicycle in this cold? The person pulled off a yellow helmet and goggles. Sunshine. Why wasn't he surprised?

He stepped out of the car and slammed the door behind him.

"It's too cold to ride a bicycle."

"My faith keeps me warm."

This was what he hated about Christians—why did they act so sanctimonious all the time?

Sunshine grimaced. "I'm sorry, I shouldn't have said that."

He nodded to acknowledge her apology.

"I don't drive. Don't know how."

He blinked at her. "You don't drive? Ever? How old are you?" He scanned her for clues. "About twenty-five?"

She propped her hands on her hips. "Didn't anybody ever tell you it's rude to ask a woman her age?"

"I didn't ask your age."

"No," she rolled her eyes. "You randomly assigned a number to me as if you'd pulled it out of a hat."

Matt clenched his teeth. Why were they having this ridiculous conversation again? And what had they been talking about? Oh, right, driving.

He scowled at her. "You're telling me you never learned to drive?"

She shrugged. "It's not a priority for me."

Matt couldn't relate. Every one of his acquaintances either had a car or was in the process of buying one.

"Why not?"

Her eyes darted to his, then away.

"My dad died in a car accident when I was five."

"Oh." He was a bully for making her feel as though she needed to drive.

"Yeah. It's one of my worst memories. We were going to get a last-minute Christmas gift for my mom. One second we were driving along the highway, and the next there were all these flashing lights. And the sounds—"

Her eyes widened. "I can't describe how horrible they were."

She'd been in the car.

"Sunshine." He clasped her icy hands in his. "I'm sorry for your loss."

"It's okay." She drew in a shuddering breath.

He didn't understand this woman. How could she remain so cheerful after such a loss? "How is it you still love Christmas?"

If his parents had died during the holidays, he'd hate it even more than he already did. She blinked up at him.

"Are you kidding?"

She plucked her hands away, and Matt felt a sense of loss. Ridiculous. He tucked his hands behind him.

"How could I not be passionate about a holiday where we celebrate what God did for humanity?" She waved a hand. "Besides, which other holiday has better music or food?"

His lips twitched. This woman saw things in a way he never could.

She thrust her shoulders back. "Let's ask the mayor to let us use the beach for our event."

"Do you want me to take the lead on this one?"

She snorted. "You'll convince the mayor to let us use the beach for free because we want to raise money for a worthy cause?"

"Uh."

"Without snarling or grouching at her?" Amusement colored her voice.

The corners of his mouth twitched, but he tightened them. "Probably not. I'll defer to your superior people skills."

Matt accompanied Sunshine into the mayor's office—a too-small room that barely contained the large desk piled high with papers.

"Excuse the mess." Madge Taylor was a matronly woman who could act in one of those seasonal movies as somebody's grandmother.

"You have ten minutes." The mayor gestured to two lopsided chairs in front of her desk. "How can I help?"

"We understand your time is valuable, Mayor Taylor," Sunshine began. "Morningside Hospital is having a fundraiser to raise money for patients in need of surgery. We're hoping to host this event at Sapphire Beach."

"And you want me to waive the fee?" Madge Taylor pursed her lips. "Why should I deprive my constituents of much-needed funds because the hospital demands it?"

"Because it's for a good cause?" Sunshine gave the mayor a bright smile.

Madge Taylor snorted. "Everyone who comes through my door wants something, preferably for free, and it's always a good cause. Why is this any different?"

"The event benefits several members of this community," Matt interjected. "People like Shantoy Ducasse, a fourteen-year-old high school student who wants to grow up to serve Orange Valley. Scoliosis hampers her chances of having the life she dreams of.

"Surgery can change her life, but she doesn't have insurance, and her parents can't afford the surgery. Even if all the doctors donated their services for free, which we're planning to do, other expenses need to be covered. This fundraiser will help with that."

Madge Taylor pursed her lips. "When is this event being held?"

"December 26."

She nodded. "I'll email the approval to you. What's the address?"

Matt gave her Turner's email.

"Next time you want to get something for free, young lady," the mayor skewered Sunshine with her gaze, "lead with a story like that."

"Yes, ma'am." Sunshine snapped a sharp salute that had Ms. Taylor's lips twitching.

As they left the mayor's office, he sensed Sunshine's gaze on him.

"What?"

"Oh, nothing." She shook her head.

He unlocked his car and gestured to her bike. "I can drop you to wherever you're going if you put that in the trunk."

"Yup." She nodded as she unlocked her bike and handed it to him. "You've confirmed my suspicion."

Matt growled. "You know our conversations would be easier if you'd speak clearly, right?" He put the bike in the trunk and held the passenger door open for her.

"You want plain speaking? Here's the truth." She grinned at him. "You, Doctor Churlish, are a fraud."

Five

Here Comes Trouble

"Today was fun." She smiled at her mom. Trixie had worked the entire day with her, reminding Sunshine of the times she'd helped in the shop during high school.

"It was." Trixie stroked a hand over her hair.

"What do you think of these ideas?" Sunshine angled the sketchpad toward her mom.

She had sketched out a couple of designs for her mother's bridal bouquet. Trixie's dress was an embroidered, long-sleeved gown with a seventies vibe that fit her mother's personality to a tee. Sunshine was leaning toward a cascade using a combination of lilies and orchids.

"Oh, I don't care." Trixie waved a hand. "Did I tell you Keith's taking me on a trip to Europe?"

Her eyebrows shot up. "No. Weren't you guys going to spend a week at a hotel in Cinnamon Hill?"

"That was the original plan." Trixie tittered. "The trip is Ian's and Marie's gift to us. Well, the members of Keith's old squad helped."

And none of her new children thought to reach out to ask if Sunshine wanted to contribute.

Let no root of bitterness spring up and cause trouble.

Sunshine squashed the jealousy threatening to choke her.

"I'm sure you guys will have fun." She tipped her lips into a smile. "How long will you be gone?"

"Two weeks." Excitement radiated off Trixie. "It's going to be perfect. When I come back, you and I will do something together. Just the two of us."

"That would be nice." Sunshine moved to stand beside Trixie in front of the counter. "There's this restaurant in Portsville you'd enjoy."

"Portsville?" Trixie's eyes met Sunshine's, her smile frozen. "Why would we drive to Portsville?"

Something told Sunshine she and her mother were no longer talking about the same thing.

"Because that's where I live?"

"Then who's going to take care of the shop?"

Sunshine shrugged. It had been a long time since she'd been responsible for the day-to-day running of The Fair Child.

"You can close the shop for two weeks."

"I can't." Trixie wailed. "We have deliveries scheduled through the new year."

Sunshine blinked. "Then who did you think would run it?"

Trixie turned to her and grabbed both of her hands. Oh no. She shook her head at her mother's plaintive expression.

"I have a job, Mom. In another city. Surely you don't expect me to quit and move back to Orange Valley?"

"Yes, that's exactly what I expect you to do." Trixie was using what Sunshine had dubbed her "Mom voice". Her mother was serious.

Sunshine gaped. "You're kidding."

"No, Sunshine. I'm not. Keith's security consulting business is taking off, and he's getting jobs all across the island. We plan to buy an RV so I can travel with him."

"You're going to sell the flower shop?" Her chest hurt at the thought.

"No. But I don't want to run it anymore." Trixie waved to encompass the shop. "The Fair Child was never my dream. It was your father's. I kept it going for you, but it's time for you to take care of your legacy."

Sunshine was still processing her mother's statement when she left to meet Zoë in town. Trixie couldn't be serious. She expected Sunshine to quit her job as one of the premier florists in Portsville to do what? Work in a flower shop?

What was the point of her going all the way to Portsville to learn floral design if she was going to return to Orange Valley to sell cut flowers and potted plants?

Sunshine locked her bike in front of Island Sound, then checked her watch. The small store had a wide variety of electronic devices and was the place Sunshine shopped when she needed a new device.

She was on time, so where was Zoë? She pulled out her cell phone and called her.

"Hello?"

The voice on the other end of the line was so rough that Sunshine pulled the phone from her ear to check the number.

"Zoë? It's Sunshine. Are you okay?"

Zoë moaned. "Sick. Asked Dr. Beckett to fill in."

Sunshine suppressed a groan, not wanting to add to the younger woman's distress.

"Don't worry about us. We'll be fine."

If one of them didn't end up killing the other.

As she ended the call, Matt strolled toward her. Why did he have to be so good-looking? Because, really, the low-cropped dirty blond hair that revealed a sexy head and killer green eyes were wasted on such a grumpy man. Especially one who doesn't believe in God. Sunshine rolled her eyes.

Matt lifted a brow. "Don't tell me I've annoyed you already?"

As if she'd admit that she'd been admiring him. She mimicked his expression.

"Don't tell me you're one of those guys who believe everyone's always thinking about them?"

His lips twisted into a crooked smile. An attractive smile that had her wishing things were different. That *he* was different.

"Only you, Sunshine. I'm sure I'm the last thing on your mind when you go to sleep and the first thing when you wake up."

She rolled her eyes again. "In case you were wondering, that one was for you."

Sunshine stomped past him and entered the electronic store. She smiled at Victor Welds.

"Hey, Victor. Is Kenny here?"

Kenny was Victor's grandson and the resident tech guy. He also moonlighted as a DJ.

"Kenny." Victor turned his head to the side and bellowed over his shoulder. "It's been a while, Sunshine."

"I was here for Easter, Vic."

"It's not the same as your being here all the time. When are you moving back home?"

She shrugged, keeping her smile firmly in place. Was this a conspiracy?

Victor cast a sly glance toward Matt. "I bet if you found the right guy, you'd move back in a jiffy."

Why did people keep hinting that Matt would be an ideal partner for her? Did they not know the man? The *real* surprise would be if anyone truly knew him since he seemed to keep everyone at a distance.

"I love my life in Portsville."

No, she didn't. The only reason she wasn't lonely was because she worked all the time. It wasn't uncommon for her to go in for a few hours on her day off. But nobody in Orange Valley needed to know that—she refused to fuel their delusions of her returning home.

"Sunny!" The former football player rushed toward her and lifted her off her feet.

"Put me down, you big oaf." Sunshine beat on Kenny's shoulders, laughing.

"Nope." He spun in a slow circle. "Not until you say Kenny is the greatest."

"No." He spun faster until she got dizzy. "Alright. Alright. Kenny is the greatest."

She clenched his shoulders until the earth stopped spinning before she released him.

"Kenny Welds is the greatest troublemaker in Orange Valley."

He grinned. "And you love him."

She grinned back at the man who'd taught her to climb trees and had been her best friend through high school.

"You know it."

* * *

Matt's hands curled into fists when the linebacker-sized man grabbed Sunshine and spun her until she laughed. Laughed. Every single time she was around him, they got into an argument, but this guy got all the sunshine.

When Kenny put her down, Matt worked at keeping his face neutral. Not that it worked because his scowl had only deepened.

"Hey." Kenny tipped his head toward him and he forced himself to do the same.

"What can I do for you, Sunny?" Kenny clasped both of her hands in his while she beamed at him. Beamed.

"I need a DJ for an event on Boxing Day, Kenny."

"Aw, Sunshine." Kenny's face fell. "You know my December dates book out months in advance."

"It's during the day." She turned to him for confirmation. He gave a curt nod.

"The event starts at ten," Matt spoke through clenched teeth, resisting the urge to growl at the man.

"Oh," Kenny dropped Sunshine's hands—finally—and rubbed his palms together. "Then I'm your man, but I gotta leave by six."

Sunshine rested a palm on the man's beefy forearm. Did Matt need arms like that for her to touch him? Why did he want her to?

Oh, man, it must be this stupid season. All those peppy Christmas songs were getting to him. Even this electronic store had gotten a copy of Mariah Carey's Christmas album, which they no doubt played on repeat.

"We can't pay you, Kenny."

"Wait. Hold up." Kenny raised both hands. "You want me to DJ an event for you, for free? In the middle of my busiest season?"

Kenny studied at them as if they were crazy, and Matt had to admit, he agreed with him. Sunshine nodded slowly.

"Sunny, you're one of my best friends, but no—"

"It's for charity. The money's going to be used to pay medical expenses for people who can't afford it. Some of them are children."

"Aw, man. Why you gotta say that?" Kenny screwed up his face.

"Because it's true." Sunshine tapped his bicep. "Why don't we barter? What task have you been putting off because you don't want to do it? We'll do it for you, and you'll DJ for us."

Kenny's gaze fluttered between him and Sunshine. "You guys will do my chores for me?"

Matt stared at Sunshine, eager for the answer as well.

"No," Sunshine held up a finger. "We'll do one chore for you."

"Alright," Kenny stroked his chin. "I can work with that. You see those Christmas trees?"

"Trees that should have been decorated a month ago." Victor groused, eliciting a grin from Sunshine.

Kenny flashed a long-suffering look at the old man. "I'm supposed to decorate them, but you know how I hate doing that."

"Yeah, you'd rather be playing music than standing still."

"Exactly. If you decorate those trees for me, you got yourself a DJ."

"Deal." Sunshine thrust out her hand and she and Kenny shook enthusiastically. "What are you doing this evening, Matt?"

"Let me guess, I'm decorating a Christmas tree."

Something he had zero experience doing. But he had no

choice. Turner had rearranged his schedule to give him time to plan the fundraiser with Sunshine since no one else had volunteered.

"It's going to be fun." Sunshine rubbed her hands together.

"Hmm," Matt flashed a glance at her. Her enthusiasm lit up a room—made him feel…something. More than he wanted to uncover at this moment or any time soon.

He shifted his attention to Kenny. The man ferried boxes from somewhere in the back of the store to the display window where the two artificial trees stood. There were a lot of boxes.

Kenny dropped a large box of decorations at the base of the smaller tree with a grunt.

"That's everything." He dusted off his hands. "Playing for free is almost worth not having to untangle a gazillion Christmas lights."

Matt grimaced. Yeah, the man had passed off his unappealing chore to him.

"Anyway, gotta go. I'm playing tonight." He hugged Sunshine. "Don't be a stranger. We still have Pizza Night on Wednesdays, if you wanna stop by." His glance cut to Matt. "Bring your bodyguard if you must."

Matt waited until after the man had left before addressing Sunshine.

"Is this what we're doing now?" He gestured to the boxes. "Doing people's disgusting chores to get them to help us?"

She plopped her hands on her hips. "Do you have another suggestion? Did the hospital approve a budget to pay for the things we'll need to put on this event?"

He rolled his lips. Why did this woman short-circuit the logical side of his brain? Everything she'd said was true and something he would have agreed with if it had been anyone but her.

"Yes, well, nobody checked if I know anything about decorating Christmas trees."

He had a vague memory of doing it with his parents, but in the years since he'd lived with his grandfather, they'd never had a tree. Nor had he owned a tree since he'd lived on his own.

"Don't worry, Doctor Glum," she patted his cheek. "I'll put those pretty surgeon hands of yours to good use."

Matt sucked in a breath as sensations washed over him. His vision narrowed to just her. What would it be like to allow himself to get lost in her caramel eyes? To tug her closer and dip his head to hers? He wanted things he couldn't have. Things he didn't deserve. Because she was right.

He was glum and grumpy, and all the adjectives she'd used to describe him. And she was sunshine. Pure and simple. A bright light that deserved more than the darkness he'd been carrying around with him for more than half his life.

He knelt and lifted the flap of the first box. "Where do we start?"

She knelt beside him. "I start with a theme." She removed ornaments from the box and put them in groups.

"What are you doing?"

"If I'm going to come up with a theme, I need to know what types of ornaments they have."

"That makes sense." He pulled items from the box and created his piles beside him.

"What?" She glanced at him. "I finally said something that made you realize I was smart?"

Matt frowned at her. "I never said you weren't smart." Where had she gotten that idea?

"Could have fooled me."

"Sunshine," he rested a hand on hers, "I never, for one second, thought you weren't smart."

Six

Shine So Bright

Matt's words loosened a knot inside Sunshine's chest. One that had tightened after she'd met her future siblings, Doctor and Doctor West. The shame of not attending college was a secret burden she lugged around all the time.

Sunshine knew she was smart enough—she had the grades to prove it and the acceptance letters from two universities. But without the funds, attending university had been out of the question. She'd settled for a short course in floral design, which had resulted in an internship at Bella Flora.

"Thanks." She tugged her hand away from his. "Guess I assumed because you were a doctor and everything," she let her words trail off. What was she going to say? She'd stuck her hangups on him and then gotten mad?

Matt smirked. "You know what they say about assumptions."

Sunshine gaped at him. "Was that a joke, Doctor?"

Had she misjudged him? Here he was, cheering her up after she'd gone off on him.

"I can do jokes." His tone remained grumpy. "I can even do knock-knock ones." He cleared his throat. "Here's one. Knock-knock."

She groaned, "Nope, I'm not doing that with you."

"Then tell me who made you believe you weren't smart enough." His eyes blazed as if he wanted to find the person responsible and give them a firm talking to.

She swallowed. Could she truly share this with him?

You can win more battles with kindness than by being antagonistic.

"No one ever told me I wasn't smart enough. It's more of a feeling." She shrugged and pointed to the group of red and white ornaments.

"Let's do one tree in the traditional colors and the other in blue and gold. Space the decorations when you hang them so we don't have any overcrowded areas."

Matt nodded and began hanging ornaments, forehead marred in concentration.

"It's this your first time decorating a Christmas tree?" He hung every ornament with precision.

"I'm not sure. My parents died when I was seven."

Her hand flew to her mouth. "Oh, Matt, I'm so sorry."

"It's okay. It happened a long time ago." He eyed the tree before hanging another ornament, using his fingers to measure the distance. "My grandfather raised me, and he wasn't one for Christmas."

He wasn't one for affectionate gestures either, if Sunshine was reading Matt right.

"So what led you to believe you weren't smart enough?"

Sunshine picked up a handful of ornaments and stood next to him. "Are you sure you didn't get a degree in psychology along with your medical one?"

He turned his green gaze on her. "Don't do that."

"What?" Her eyebrows shot up in genuine curiosity.

"Don't make light of your feelings, as if they're not worth anything. I may not have studied psychology, but I've witnessed the impact of what people believe about themselves manifest in their bodies.

"I've seen people with illnesses that were not life-threatening worry themselves to death in weeks."

He buttoned his lips and took a few deep breaths. "So, I'll ask you again, Sunshine, what caused you to believe you weren't smart enough?"

Was she doing that? Making light of her feelings? Hadn't her mother said something similar?

"Do you know what it's like having the friends you helped study move on to university while you're left behind?"

Most of the time, the separation was permanent, as some pretended not to know her when they came back from university. If they came back.

"No." Matt's voice was full of empathy.

"Well, it stinks, especially when you bump into the ones who love to gloat about their accomplishments."

Like the former classmate whose wedding flowers she'd done last month.

"I met my fiance in college." Sunshine mimicked the woman's nasal tone. "Do you remember Harry? You didn't go to school with us, did you?"

It seemed as if she had some residual anger, after all.

"Hmm," Matt grunted, "Half the people who go to university

are idiots. The other half are fools."

She grinned. "Which one are you, Doctor Broody?"

"I'm a rarity," his green eyes met hers, "I somehow manage to be both."

Her amusement dried up at his expression. It was as if Matt saw past all her defenses to the woman she was inside. Was her mother right? Was she using cheerfulness as a shield?

"Uh—"

"Don't let anybody cause you to forget your worth, Sunshine. Some people are unhappy despite the image they portray. They'd want nothing more than to make you as unhappy as they are."

Was he talking about himself?

* * *

Matt turned away from the sympathy in Sunshine's eyes. Except for Ian and Marie, he never exposed his feelings. Why was he doing it to a woman who'd made it clear how she despised his stance on religion?

He broke eye contact. "What happens now?"

"Now—"

His gaze returned to her face without his consent. He should stop staring at Sunshine. What was her last name, anyway?

"What's your full name?"

She smirked at him. "Suppose I'm one of those single-name people?"

"Are you?"

"I'll never tell."

"Alright." He was enjoying bantering with her. "I'll just give you my surname." His face warmed. "I-I mean, I'll make up a name for you."

"I got it, Doctor Glum." She burst into laughter. "You should have seen your face."

"Let's string these lights." He grabbed the first strand and pretended to know what he was doing.

About an hour into his tree decorating, Matt started singing along with the soundtrack in his head.

"No."

"Are you alright?" Sunshine peered around the tree at him.

Had he spoken aloud?

"I'm fine." He bit the word off.

"You're talking to yourself."

"No. I'm talking to the person who wrote this stupid song that I've somehow memorized."

She giggled. Her name wasn't so silly after all. Because if he had to assign an image to the sound of her laugh, it would be sunshine. Bright days filled with laughter and fun.

Had he ever had days like that? He had a vague memory of playing in a field and frowned. Was that a memory of him and his parents? There were so few of them that Matt could no longer determine what was memory and what was imagination.

In less time than he'd thought possible, Sunshine stopped to examine the trees.

"I think it's time for us to put the stars on the tops." She headed toward the counter. "I'll go check if Victor has a ladder."

She returned in a few minutes. "Good news and bad news."

Matt frowned. Why did people do that? The good news was never enough to outweigh the bad.

"The good news is he has a ladder. The bad news is that he loaned it out," she smiled up at him. "You wouldn't want to come back another day to finish up, would you?"

And watch her and Kenny make cow eyes at each other? Not a chance.

He stepped back and studied the tree. His gaze scanned her from head to toe.

"What are you thinking?" She narrowed her eyes at him. "Something tells me I won't like it."

"Well," he stroked his chin. "There's a way we can finish up today."

"Really?" Her eyes lit up. "How?"

Did she know how beautiful she was? And he had no right to think anything about how she looked.

"I can lift you." He ran his gaze over her frame. "What are you? About one-fifty?"

She snorted. "A woman never tells her weight. Didn't your grandfather tell you that?"

"My grandfather and I didn't discuss those types of things."
"Oh."

There was that expression of pity again.

"Are we doing this or not?"

She grabbed the first star. "We're doing it." She grasped the star with both hands. "How do we do this? Do I clamber onto your back or what?"

"Stay still," he squatted beside her, grabbing her legs as he rose to his full height.

"Matt!" she squealed, clutching his shoulders.

"Hang the star, Sunshine." He enjoyed having her in his arms way too much.

Seven

Christmas Dilemma

Sunshine used her phone to search for verses on temptation, jotting down the ones that resonated in her Bible study notebook. She needed help to resist the temptation Matt presented. The more she spent time with him, the more convinced she became that her mother was right. Again.

Matt's disbelief in God came from a place of hurt. If she had to guess the source, she'd point fingers at his grandfather. She'd never met the man and already believed he was cold and unfeeling.

It must have been difficult for a child to live with him, especially one who'd lost both his parents.

"God, I need You to tell me what to do."

"Everything okay?" Trixie shuffled into the room wearing a bathrobe.

"Everything's fine." Things had been tense between them

since her mother dropped her bombshell. It still boggled her mind that Trixie expected Sunshine to quit her job and move to Orange Valley to take over the shop.

"Aren't you supposed to be getting ready for work?"

Trixie's eyebrow raised. "Me? Aren't you working this morning?"

Sunshine searched her memory for any conversation they'd had about making a switch. "No. You didn't say anything to me."

"Can you be a dear and open the shop this morning?" Trixie pouted. "Keith wants to take me out for breakfast."

"No." Sunshine stared at the woman in front of her. Trixie Fairchild had never flaked on work. What was going on with her mother? Sunshine slapped her notebook shut and stood. "Why are you acting this way?"

"Like what?" Trixie batted innocent eyes at her.

"A flake." Her mom may have an issue with being on time in her personal life, but she kept her commitments. In all the years she'd been running The Fair Child, she'd opened the store on time.

Trixie sighed. "You're right. I'm sorry."

Her mother shucked off her bathrobe to reveal her dusty pink uniform. The color had changed since her father's death, but the design and logo remained the same.

Sunshine cocked her head. "What was this? A test?"

"Sort of." Trixie rolled her eyes. "Not really. I am serious about you taking over the running of the shop, though."

"You *can't* be. Where would I live?"

Trixie shrugged. "You'd live here, of course. I'm moving in with Keith."

Why were they having this conversation again? And, so soon.

"Mom, I live in Portsville. You're asking me to quit my job and move my belongings back home so I can replace you at the shop—with no advance notice."

"Oh, please, I've been dropping hints for years. Is this the first time I've said the words out loud?"

"Yes!"

Her mother had blindsided her.

"Honey," Trixie rested a hand on Sunshine's arms. "This may seem like the last thing you want to do, but is the life you have in Portsville the one you want?"

"Of course it is. I love my life." And the best way to convince herself and everyone else was to be insistent and loud about it.

"No, you don't." Trixie shook her head. "You're overworked and isolated. You don't have any friends and never go out for fun. And on the days you should be in church, you're too exhausted to attend."

This was the problem with treating your mother as if she were your best friend—she knew all your secrets.

"Mom," Sunshine's voice was plaintive. "I worked hard to get where I was. Aren't you the one who always encouraged me to improve my skills?"

Ever since the first time she'd attempted to create a bouquet for someone to gift to his wife when she'd been in high school.

"You've done that. Now it's time to come home and use those skills here."

"Doing what?"

Trixie shrugged. "I'm not sure, but I've been praying about this for a year, and this is what I believe the Lord wants me to do."

Her mom had been praying about the shop for an entire year and hadn't mentioned it before this week?

"What happens if I don't want to move back to Orange Valley?"

"Then we need to decide if we'll hire someone to manage it, or sell the shop."

Sunshine gasped. "What about the house?"

She'd grown up here. The doorjamb in the kitchen had the marks that her mother used to measure her height.

"I don't know." Trixie met her gaze. "I'd keep it for a while, but eventually we'd have to decide what to do about that, too."

Her mother's meaning was clear. If Sunshine didn't take over The Fair Child, they'd not only lose the shop but their house as well.

Hire someone to manage it or sell the shop.

The words reverberated through Sunshine's mind as she ducked into Daisy's room. The thought of selling The Fair Child tore her to pieces. Her mom had told her countless times about her father's dream of owning a flower shop.

Her love for flowers had flourished out of her mother's stories. For Sunshine, they were a way to connect with her father.

The Fair Child was his legacy—one she'd believed would always be around. Yet, one she had never considered as part of *her* legacy. Even the potential loss of her childhood home didn't hurt as much as losing the flower shop.

A good man leaveth an inheritance to his children's children.

Wasn't that how it was supposed to work? Parents left things for their children to inherit. But what happens when the children don't want the legacy the parents have built up for them?

"Is everything okay with you, Sunshine?" Daisy's brow furrowed in concern. "Your smile doesn't quite fill your eyes today."

"I was just thinking."

"About what, dear?"

"Nothing." She shook her head, though the desire to fill Daisy's ears with her trouble was almost irresistible. "I don't want to burden you."

"You won't burden me. Come," Daisy held out a hand. "The Lord never meant for us to carry our burdens all by ourselves."

"Bear ye one another's burdens, and so fulfill the law of Christ."

"Exactly!" Daisy beamed at her. "Tell this old woman your troubles and let me help you bear some of the weight."

At Daisy's encouragement, Sunshine spilled her mother's request along with how unfulfilled she'd been at her job in recent months.

"I never considered running The Fair Child, but I'm not sure if I want to return to the frantic pace of life in Portsville."

Being in Orange Valley had reminded her how much she loved connecting with others. Had she been in Portsville, the only people she'd be spending time with would either be coworkers or clients. While she loved her job and liked most of her co-workers, was that what life was all about? Work?

Daisy patted her hand, drawing Sunshine's attention back to her. "Sounds to me as if the Lord's already showing you your next step."

Sunshine straightened in the chair. "What do you mean?"

"In my experience," Daisy spoke slowly, "God has a way of making you uncomfortable in your current situation when it's time for you to move on to the next thing."

"I don't understand." Was Daisy agreeing with her mother, telling Sunshine she should quit her job and move back home?

Daisy pressed her lips together, and Sunshine hoped the older woman's next words would contain the pearls of wisdom she needed.

Please, Lord. Give Daisy the right words so I can understand.

"You said the job wasn't as fun as it had been when you first started. Is that true?"

Sunshine nodded.

"And that you've been wanting a change?"

Well, she hadn't said those exact words, but the truth of them sunk into her spirit.

"Yes."

Daisy stroked the back of Sunshine's hand. "God's trying to get your attention. Do you believe He goes before you and makes your path straight?"

"Of course." It was something she loved about being a believer—knowing she was never alone.

"Then the discomfort you're feeling in your position at…"

"Bella Flora."

"Discomfort may be a sign that it's time for you to move into the next phase of your journey."

Daisy patted her hand. "Pray about it, dear, and be willing to listen to the answer, even if you don't like what God is telling you."

* * *

Matt spotted a flash of yellow as he left the hospital room of his last patient of the day. Sunshine. Why his brain now associated the color with her was no surprise. Every time they'd met, she wore at least one article of clothing in some shade of the color. He lengthened his stride to catch up with her.

Her accusation from the night he'd had dinner with her and her family flashed through her mind. He wasn't stalking her. Exactly. He was providing a timely update. She pushed through the main door.

"Sunshine."

His shout garnered a bit more attention than he'd have liked, but she stopped, one hand on the door.

He closed the distance between them.

"Why Doctor Crabby, if I didn't know better, I'd believe you were excited to see me."

More than he would admit. After someone bumped into him for the third time, he pulled her away from the exit.

"I have updates."

"Oh, good." Her lips formed a smile, but the light in her eyes remained dim.

"What's wrong?" His eyes scanned her features for any sign that she might need medical attention.

"Nothing." Her smile widened.

"No. Something's wrong." He tipped her chin up. "Your eyes aren't smiling."

"I'm going to get me a pair of shades. Why's everybody always staring into my eyes?"

He bit back a smile. "Maybe it's the color. At the right angle, they're like caramel."

She blinked. Had he managed to silence her? Good.

"I was about to get something to eat." He thumbed over his shoulder. "Have dinner with me?"

"I don't know." She gnawed at her bottom lip, and Matt made a point of focusing on her eyes so he wouldn't get distracted. She had kissable lips.

"It depends on what you plan to eat."

"I'm in the mood for pasta." It was the closest restaurant to the hospital, and they'd have privacy. "Plus, I have updates." He arranged his fingers into the scout's symbol. "You can consider it a working dinner."

"Okay, Doctor Grump. I'll have dinner with you."

Matt opened the door for her, ignoring the staff gawking at them. He waited until the server had settled their meals before them and she'd taken her first bite.

"Why do you have sad eyes?"

Sunshine chewed slowly, glaring at him the entire time. She swallowed. "What's this fascination you have with my eyes?"

Did he tell her that sometimes her eyes made him forget what he was thinking? Or that he could stare into them for hours? Probably not the answer she was expecting.

He twirled a forkful of pasta. "You can't have a name like Sunshine and be sad."

She sighed and put the fork down. "My mother wants me to move back to Orange Valley and take over The Fair Child."

"The Fair Child?"

"My family's flower shop."

"And you don't want to do it." It was a statement. Her reluctance was etched in every fiber of her being.

"I'm not sure what I want." She moved the salt and pepper shakers around on the table. "I thought it was to keep working at Bella Flora, but now I don't know."

"What's holding you back from taking over your family's flower shop?"

"I love making floral arrangements." Her face lit up. "Since I've been here, I can count on one hand the number of times someone wanted something other than potted plants, cut flowers, or a simple bouquet."

"So?" He motioned for her to continue.

"What was the point of all my training and experience if I don't use them?" Sunshine's anguish was genuine, and he was determined not to disregard her feelings.

What if someone asked him to stop practicing medicine to do something that didn't require any of the skills he'd acquired? How would he have felt? What would he have done?

He allowed himself to imagine it for a moment. He loved being a doctor. For him, it was about improving the quality of someone's life. What if he was asked to give that up and do something else?

"Cat got your tongue, Doctor?" Sunshine smirked at him.

"I'm giving your question the proper consideration." He met her gaze. "I don't understand the difference between your old job and your mother's expectations, but you can make some changes, right?

"Can't you include more of what you love in your family's flower shop? Or find out what other flower shops in the area do that are more in line with what you did in Portsville."

She jolted. "You're right." She scooped up a forkful of pasta while her eyes danced. "There's a shop on the other side of town." Her brow furrowed. "Something or other Garden. It's a fairy tale character."

"Pinocchio? Rapunzel? Rumpelstiltskin?"

She arched a brow. "Are you sprouting off names of random characters?"

"Yes." His lips quirked. "Not helping?"

"Not one bit. It's okay. I'll research it when I get home."

"Or," he slid his phone from his pocket, "we can google it now."

He searched for florists in Orange Valley, scanning the list for names that included the word garden, and that could have belonged to a fairy tale character.

"Is it Belle's Garden?"

"That's it!"

Her smile warmed him from the inside. He rubbed his chest to dispel the sensation.

"Glad to help." His gaze dropped to the plate in front of him. He enjoyed being with Sunshine way too much.

"You promised me updates." She jabbed a fork at him, "Spill."

"I got confirmation on three bachelors for the auction you plan to host at the fundraiser."

He'd growled at them and applied a heavy layer of guilt until they'd agreed, but she didn't need to know his tactics.

"Sweet." Sunshine gave him a mini round of applause. "Now all we have to do are a gazillion other things before time runs out, and we'll be fine."

She seemed delighted at the prospect, whereas he was reluctant for their time together to end. If only there was a way to slow the clock to extend their time together as long as possible.

Eight

Apologies, Prayers, and Confessions

"Those are lovely." Marie nodded to the small bouquets Sunshine had completed. She'd considered Matt's suggestion and created a few simple arrangements to determine if there was a market for them.

"Thank you." Sunshine stashed the bouquets in the fridge before returning to the other woman. "How may I help?"

She'd promised her mother to spend time with her future in-laws. But planning the fundraiser was taking more time than she'd anticipated.

Marie glanced around the shop before leaning closer to Sunshine and lowering her voice. "Your mom doesn't want a bachelorette party, but Ian and I were thinking we should still do something for her."

Hadn't a trip to Europe been enough?

Let no root of bitterness spring up and cause trouble.

She blew out a breath and focused on keeping calm. Her

mother deserved to be happy.

"Okay."

Marie stared at Sunshine with an eager expression. Did she expect Sunshine to come up with an idea on the spot?

"What was your idea?"

"We don't have any. That's one reason I'm here." Marie huffed. "Ian and I are both only children, but we've always wanted a sister."

Sunshine arched a brow. Where was this going?

"We should've reached out to you when we gifted Keith and Trixie with the trip to Europe."

"Did Mom say something to you?" She thought she'd done an excellent job of keeping her emotions under wraps.

"No." Marie half-smiled. "Both of us are psychologists, and…"

Sunshine nodded, doing her best to picture her calming field of sunflowers. She did not want this woman picking up things from her body language that she had no intention of saying aloud.

"We realized later we'd crossed several boundaries by doing that." Marie scratched at the counter. "Although we probably learned that from all the research we've been doing into blended families."

Listen to her heart.

It was tempting for Sunshine to pull away from this woman. The one with her degree in psychology and who knows what kind of accolades. Was there something else going on here?

She scanned the woman in a pair of jeans and a thick sweater. With her hair loose around her face, she wasn't coming at Sunshine from a place of superiority. Instead, she'd admitted to making a mistake and had approached her for a way forward.

In her opinion, Ian should have been the one here, but that was out of her control. Besides, since Marie and Ian were married, the two had become one. Maybe that's how it worked with married couples.

"Does Ian know you're here?"

Marie nodded. "He's waiting in the car. We thought it would be easier for you if the request came from me."

Not really, all he'd done was pass off his responsibility to someone else. Still, she could take offense, or accept the gesture for what it was—an apology.

She rested her hand on top of Marie's. "I've always wanted a sister, too."

"How about a brother?"

Sunshine's eyes flitted up to Ian, who'd snuck into the store while her attention was fixed on Marie.

His expression was hopeful. "Please tell me you'd like to have a brother because I have all these things I'd like to do for a little sister."

Sunshine grinned as her heart eased. She'd been ready to get upset at the couple, but God had already gone before and put His plan in place.

"I can get used to the idea of a big brother, although I can't imagine what kinds of things you plan to do with a full-grown sister."

Ian waggled his eyebrows. "Oh, the ideas I've come up with will surprise you."

Sunshine groaned and covered her face with her hand. "Is it too late to be placed with a foster family?"

"You'll be fine." Marie patted Sunshine's hand. "I'll keep him in check for you."

"So," Ian rubbed his hands together. "What are we doing for

a bachelorette party?"

Sunshine ran through several possibilities. She may not have been a wedding planner, but she'd attended lots of weddings and wedding-related events.

"What if, instead of a party, we have an intimate dinner instead? One where we play games, and have a few," she cast her eyes at her future in-laws, "small gifts."

"Can we make it family only?" Ian raised his eyebrows at her. "That works."

She should get used to more people being in her family. Would they invite Matt to join them? If her heart beat a little faster at the thought, she'd never admit it.

* * *

Matt stood beside his patient's bed. John Ennis had slipped into a coma earlier that day after the team believed his condition was improving.

None of the tests explained why his health was declining. Matt clenched his fists at his impotence. They didn't teach this in medical school—how helpless you'd feel when you've followed all the procedures and the patient didn't improve as expected.

He smelled Sunshine's distinct floral scent before she crept up beside him.

"We've done everything, but instead of improving, his condition keeps getting worse."

"I'm sorry."

He believed her. Sometimes when people said those two words, it was more routine than anything, but Sunshine's compassion pulsed off her.

"I—" she shifted her weight from one foot to the other.

Matt turned his full attention to her. Sunshine had never been this ill at ease around him.

"What is it?"

"Is it okay if I pray for him?"

He scoffed. "Prayer? That's your solution?"

She flinched. He lowered his voice when what he wanted to do was bellow his rage.

"Scores of the best doctors have studied his case. We've run every test imaginable and can't identify what's causing the issue or how to help him."

Prayer hadn't helped his parents. Dozens of people had prayed for them. But they'd still been severely beaten and had succumbed to their injuries.

Sunshine rested a hand on his. "You may not believe in God, but you've tried everything else." She shrugged. "It can't hurt."

When she put it that way, she had a point. "Guess not."

"Thank you." She squeezed his hand before stepping closer to John. "What's his name?"

Matt cleared his throat. "John."

Sunshine nodded to acknowledge him. Her lips moved silently, and Matt was a bit disappointed. Surely, she'd want to pray aloud.

As if in response to his thoughts, she began speaking.

"Abba Father, I put Your son John into Your hands. The doctors don't know what's wrong with him, but You do. Even better, You're the Great Physician and can heal him.

"Father, this is an opportunity to show Your glory so that the medical staff will know that You're alive and powerful. Place Your hands on John and restore his health. In Your name, I pray. Amen."

For a moment after Sunshine had finished praying, there was a hush, as if something supernatural hovered in the air. But that was foolish, wasn't it? Because even if there was a God, he was too busy to concern himself with him and John, wasn't he?

Matt shook off the strange mood. "What happens now?"

Sunshine met his gaze. "We wait."

He gaped at her, "That's it? John won't miraculously awaken from his coma?"

She shrugged. "He might. Or he may gradually recover. Or," her lips quivered into a sad smile, "he may not."

"What's the point of believing in God if he doesn't perform a miracle when you ask him to?"

"God isn't a circus monkey, Matt. He's capable of doing things we can't imagine. And sometimes He does them, but He does everything in *His* timing and according to *His* will."

He didn't get it. Wasn't that why people believed? Because it guaranteed that life would work out better for them than for people who didn't believe?

"Isn't being a believer like being in a secret club? Aren't there benefits?"

"It is and there are, but not how you're thinking." She tapped her chin. "When we choose Christ, we become enemies of the devil who'll do anything to destroy us."

He grimaced. "Why would anyone want to do something that nets them an adversary?"

"Because the benefits are far greater." Her eyes shone. "Don't you see? With God on our side, we can do so much more. We have more joy, peace, love. Hope."

Hope. Did he know what that felt like? Optimism, yes, but did he believe in anything that lit him up from the inside the way Sunshine's faith in God lit her up?

"The best thing is being in a relationship with God, and knowing we can count on Him."

"Aren't there hoops you have to jump through? Don't you get kicked out of his good graces if you make a mistake?"

"Oh, Matt." Compassion filled Sunshine's eyes. "There's no mistake we can make that God's grace doesn't cover."

Had he misunderstood what Christianity was about all this time? Could it be less about performance and good deeds and more about relationships?

If it was, it meant his grandfather had been wrong. And if Alan Beckett had been wrong about God, what else had he been wrong about?

"Why are you so resistant to prayer?"

Sunshine's soft question jolted him back to the present. Matt's eyes darted around the room.

"Not here." He touched her arm, needing the warmth of human contact. "Can we go somewhere?" The need to share his past with someone—with Sunshine—was almost overwhelming.

"Sure." She fell in step with him as he left the hospital.

"Where's your bike?"

She pointed, and they retrieved it and stashed it in the trunk. They remained quiet as Matt drove to Apple Valley Park. It was the first place that came to mind. He spared a glance at Sunshine, who was content to remain silent. How had he ever thought communicating with her was hard?

The cold air stung his face as he helped Sunshine out of the car, but he needed to be moving around as he told this story.

"Are you warm enough?"

"Yes." She stuck both hands under her burgundy sweater. She peered up at him in concern. "Are you okay, Matt?"

"This is how I know you're concerned—you haven't called me Doctor Grump or any other variation today."

She half-smiled. "I'll be happy to resume my name-calling once I'm sure you're okay."

"Thanks." He brushed a hand over her hair, surprised at how soft the curls were.

"Matt." She took a step back.

He withdrew his hand. "Sorry."

He shouldn't have touched her, shouldn't have hinted that his feelings for her had shifted into something more. He gestured to the park before them. "Can we walk?"

She fell in step beside him, careful to keep distance between them. What would it be like to tuck her against his side? To link his fingers with hers and draw her close to him?

He shook his head to dispel the images that would never happen in a thousand years.

"Back at the hospital, you asked why I was resistant to prayer." He cleared his throat. "I wasn't always."

Her head swiveled toward him. "You weren't?"

"I spent my early years in the church. My parents were devout Christians. If there was an event at church, they were there." His lips quirked at the memory.

"What happened?" Her voice was devoid of judgment, which made continuing easier.

"There was a mission trip. My parents believed it was something they needed to do. I didn't go with them because they didn't want to pull me out of school."

That memory remained crystal clear when he'd forgotten so many things about them.

"They never made it back. On their last mission, a group of anti-Christians attacked them. "Six people went on the trip to proclaim the gospel. Only one person made it back."

He stopped and turned to her. "The entire church was praying for them, Sunshine. Why didn't God protect them?"

Nine

Searching for Peace

Matt turned to Sunshine with devastation in his eyes. Her heart broke for the man before her and for the boy who'd gotten the news that his parents weren't coming home.

"I don't know why God didn't answer the church's prayers for protection, Matt. But I believe He can redeem your parents' deaths for good."

He scoffed. "That's your answer?"

She flung her arms wide. "What did you expect me to say? I'm not God. I don't understand why He allows bad things to happen. All I can do is believe God is good. I choose to believe that even the hard times can become marvelous in His hands."

"Choice? That's what it comes down to?"

"Yes, Matt, choice." She poked him in the chest. "Those people *chose* to hurt your parents. They could've decided they didn't want to hear the gospel and walked away. They could've accepted the truth and surrendered their lives to Christ.

"They had a choice. Just as you had one when you sided with the people who killed your parents."

He scowled at her. "What a horrible thing to say."

Maybe. "It's true." She held up a hand to stem the words brewing in his eyes.

"An appalling thing happened to your parents and the other people on that mission trip. I get that. But when you decided God was not good and turned your back on Him, you aligned yourself with the people who killed your parents because they didn't want to believe.

"There are only two sides, Matt, and I'm sorry to tell you this, but you chose the wrong one."

Sunshine stalked away from him. When she got back to the car, she stopped. She'd been foolish. Her only mode of transportation was in Matt's car—the man she'd truth-bombed and left behind.

Why, oh, why had she felt the need to bludgeon him over the head with her opinion? She sighed. If she hurried, she wouldn't freeze to death before she got a taxi. She started plodding toward home. A few minutes later, when Matt's car pulled up beside her, she got in without a word.

She stole a glance at him. His jaw was clenched, the scowl on his face deeper than usual. Had she said the right thing?

What if, instead of inspiring him to think of the choices that had led to the place where he claimed not to believe in God, she'd pushed him further into apostasy?

Sunshine tucked her hands under her sweater and linked her fingers.

You can win more battles with kindness than by being antagonistic.

Lord, I spoke out of turn. I didn't mean to push Matt or to say things that would cause him to further pull away from You, but God, if he could only see...

If he could only see how good You are. How much You love him—I truly believe he'd choose You again. Please soften his heart so he can hear the words I intended to say instead of the ones I did.

When Matt pulled up in front of her mother's house and got her bike from the trunk, Sunshine slipped out of the car. Usually, she'd wait for him to open the door. Not tonight.

She took the handlebars from him. "I'm—"

Matt held up a hand. "You've said quite enough today, thank you. I can't handle any more of your truths."

Sunshine nodded, angling her head so he wouldn't glimpse the moisture in her eyes. She crept into the house, wanting to get to her room before the tears fell. Hopefully, her mother was out with Keith. The two were gone so often that they reminded Sunshine of a younger couple.

"Sunny?" Her mother's cheerful voice called from the kitchen as she trekked across the living room.

Sunshine knuckled away her tears. This must be one of those prayers God wouldn't answer in the affirmative.

She plastered a smile on her face and pictured speaking to a panicked bride on her wedding day. Artificial cheerfulness was often enough to suffice.

"I thought we'd spend this evening together, watching Christmas movies before things get hectic." Trixie came into the living room and stumbled to a halt. "What's wrong?"

What was the point of building up a facade of cheerfulness if everybody could detect that it wasn't real?

"Sunshine?" Trixie's eyes were full of concern.

Her resolve crumbled. "Oh, Mom, I've made everything

worse."

She allowed Trixie to draw her into a hug, resting her cheek on her mother's shoulder. What would she have done if she'd lost her mother, as well as her father? The way Matt had.

She'd been horrible to him. How dare she accuse him of siding with his parents' attackers?

"Okay, Sunshine, what happened?"

She curled up on the living room couch, her hands wrapped around a cup of hot cocoa she didn't want. She recounted Matt's confession about his parents' deaths and how she'd attacked him.

Trixie grimaced when she repeated what she'd said to Matt. Sunshine put the cup on the center table and covered her face with her hands.

"I know, Mom. I was a beast." She peered at Trixie from between her fingers. "Suppose this was the proof Matt needed to completely wall himself away from everyone?" Especially her.

"Sunny." Trixie pried Sunshine's fingers away from her face and clutched them between hers. "You give yourself too much credit."

"What do you mean?"

"What you told Matt was right. Everyone has a choice—though you could have been kinder in your delivery. Remember what we talked about?"

Her shoulder sagged. "You can win more battles with kindness than by being antagonistic."

She'd messed up. Why was she such a wonderful Christian in her head, but a poor one in real life? "What do I do now, Mom?"

"Nothing." Trixie's thumb moved in soothing circles on the

back of her hand. "Give him the chance to process what you said."

"But—"

Trixie arched a brow. "Did you expect Matt to respond to his challenges the way you do?"

"No, of course not." Sunshine stiffened her spine.

Trixie's eyes probed hers. "Are you sure?"

She hadn't done that, had she? She hadn't expected him to stop talking to her, but that didn't mean she'd thought he'd break out into a song and dance, either.

"Elena, you're one of the sweetest people in the world. You have an amazing ability to bounce back when life throws you a challenge. Not everyone is like that.

"Some of us have to sit with the hard time a bit before we can find the joy. We have to work through the pain and feel every second before we can move on to the next thing."

Sunshine frowned. "We?"

Was her mother suggesting that she also had to work through her sorrows, whereas Sunshine didn't? Hadn't she learned that behavior from her mother?

Wasn't her mom the one who'd told her stories about her dad and kept his memory alive so Sunshine didn't forget him? Wasn't it Trixie who'd taught her to choose joy?

Trixie held Sunshine's hands tighter. "When Steven died, it was the worst thing that had ever happened to me. I wanted to pull the sheets over my head and cry for a week."

The corner of her mother's mouth quivered into a sad smile.

"But I had this impressionable five-year-old who needed me to be strong. She'd gone through a traumatic event and lost her father in the process. She needed me to show her that life still had beauty."

Trixie's fingers trembled in hers. "I needed her to find the joy when things got hard. So I mourned my husband in the quiet hours at night when I was alone and celebrated his life during the daytime."

Sunshine reeled from her mother's confession. She'd always believed her mother endured her pain by choosing joy, but that had been an act.

"You lied to me." Every memory she had of Christmas was now tainted.

"No, sweet girl, I chose to celebrate my husband's life rather than focus on his death."

There was that word again—choice. It was becoming a four-letter word, one she wished didn't exist.

She tugged her fingers away from Trixie's and grabbed the cup of tea that remained unappetizing. "I don't want to talk about this anymore."

"Sunshine—"

She shook her head. Did the nickname Sunshine still fit? How could it when so many things she'd believed about herself had turned out to be false?

* * *

Matt knocked on his grandfather's front door with a minute to spare before their weekly dinner. He'd considered canceling, especially since his grandfather had asked him to come a day early. In the end, showing up was easier than suffering through a lecture.

Besides, he had questions, and the only person who could answer them was Alan Beckett.

His grandfather harrumphed. Matt followed him into the

house, registering the cavern-like interior. Had the place always been this gloomy?

He followed Alan to the small dining room table set for two and took the place on his grandfather's left. It was the place he'd always occupied, even before his parents' deaths. His father had sat opposite his grandfather, Matt's mother, to Alan's right.

The meal was always the same, too—well-done steaks, mashed potatoes, boiled carrots, and green beans.

The second Matt sat, Alan began asking about his cases. While Matt didn't provide personal information, it was something they'd always done.

The routine had begun when Matt moved in with his grandfather. Alan would share the patient's symptoms and challenge Matt to come up with a diagnosis. They'd been doing that long before Matt expressed an interest in medicine.

He tilted his head. Had he ever had a choice? Or had Alan groomed him to follow in his footsteps? In his father's? What would he have become if he'd had the option to determine where his interests lay?

"Are you listening to me?"

His grandfather's brusque voice cut into Matt's musings.

"Did Dad always want to become a doctor?"

It was the first time in memory that he'd ignored his grandfather's questions. Alan sliced into his steak, not saying a word. Had Alan heard him? Or was this his grandfather's way of ignoring him?

"Your father wanted to become a preacher, but I got that out of him."

Matt jolted. His dad had wanted to study theology?

"Told him if he was going to college on my dime, he'd study what I wanted him to."

Why was he surprised? Hadn't he gotten a version of that same speech? Except he hadn't wanted to study anything else. But maybe his grandfather had gotten better at seeding his wishes in Matt's life.

"Why didn't you want him to become a pastor?"

Alan glared at him. "Do you know what pastors earn? It's one of the worst paying jobs, especially considering everything they have to put up with."

This was about money? Matt narrowed his eyes. "Was that the real reason?"

His grandfather had accepted some unlikely items as payment during his time as a family doctor. While he was good at collecting his fees, he'd also accepted quite a few patients who couldn't pay.

Alan stuffed a bite into his mouth, scowling at Matt the whole time. Matt put down his fork, laying aside the pretense of eating.

After several moments, Alan sighed and did the same.

"What was so wrong about becoming a pastor?"

He seldom pressed his grandfather for answers. He'd learned at a young age that Alan disliked having his authority questioned. His grandfather had never hit him, but Alan sometimes went days without speaking, which for Matt had been unbearable. Until he'd learned to appreciate silence, and then to replicate it.

"I'm not the biggest fan of a god who only answers prayers when he pleases."

Matt gaped at Alan. That's it? His grandfather had forced his father to give up his dream because God hadn't answered his prayers?

"What prayer didn't He answer for you?"

Alan resumed eating as if Matt hadn't spoken. He searched his memory for everything he remembered about his family.

"Is this because Grandma died?"

Lois Beckett had died from a heart attack a few months before his parents' deaths.

"Your grandmother went to church every week. Got up every morning and prayed. What was the point of all that devotion if her God couldn't save her when she was about to die?"

"He didn't help my parents either, and they were devout Christians. In my experience, faith doesn't help anyone. I had to grow up in foster care. The only thing that benefits us in this life is hard work and dedication."

Sunshine's words came back to him.

"Maybe it wasn't that God couldn't save Grandma or your parents, but that He wanted to use their deaths for good."

He and his grandfather had more in common than he would have guessed. His grandfather's scowl made Matt want to drop the conversation. Almost. But he'd lived too long without having this wound cauterized, and it had festered.

"Did any good come out of Lois's death? Or out of Al's or Clarissa's?"

Probably not. But had that been their fault? They'd held on to the pain of their family members' deaths instead of releasing it so they could have been healed.

"We didn't give it a chance, did we?"

"You believe I made the wrong choice?" Alan thumped his fists on the table so hard that the cutlery clinked against the plates.

"Tell me how you'd react if you'd lost your wife, son, and daughter-in-law in the same year. What choices would you have made?"

Matt's chest tightened at his grandfather's words. It was the first outburst he'd ever witnessed from the man. He'd assumed his grandfather was impersonal—except when dealing with his patients.

But that hadn't been it at all. Alan had stuffed all his emotions inside and quietly demanded that Matt do the same.

Matt may not have lost his wife and children, but he'd lost his grandmother and parents. In some ways, he'd lost his grandfather as well.

"I lost them too." He kept his voice low. "I also lost the option to lean on God during the hard times instead of pulling away from Him."

His grandfather reeled back. "You're talking to me about God? What has he ever done for you?"

Matt wasn't sure how to answer that question. If Sunshine were here, she'd have a million things to say. But he wasn't Sunshine. He didn't have her experiences. Matt pushed back from the table.

"What have *we* ever done for *Him*?"

For most of his life, he'd put God in a box—ascribing to Him the attributes of a puppeteer. God pulled the strings, and everyone danced to His tune. Wasn't that what he and his dad had done regarding Alan Beckett?

His grandfather huffed and puffed, and they'd danced to his tune. Giving up their dreams or their faith because it was easier than fighting for it. No more.

Matt wanted to decide what he believed about God for himself. Without Alan Beckett Senior or the tragedy of his parents' deaths getting in the way.

"Where are you going?"

"To find some answers." Maybe Sunshine could answer them

for him…No. He would stay away from her until he figured out where he was going.

Sunshine had too much of an effect on him, and he refused to give anybody else that power over him until he'd made his peace with God.

Ten

A Christmas Miracle

Why had she agreed to help the hospital plan their stupid fundraiser? If she hadn't, she wouldn't have to meet with the administrator to give him an update. She wouldn't have to steel herself to see Matt again.

If she'd kept her mouth shut yesterday and hadn't bludgeoned the man over the head with her beliefs, she wouldn't be uncomfortable now. If only Zoë weren't still sick, she'd at least have a buffer between her and Matt.

Please, God, don't let him show up.

A short, squat man with a shiny pate approached Sunshine, his hand outstretched.

"Jack Turner, Ms. Fairchild, nice to meet you." The man scanned the narrow hallway. "Where's Dr. Beckett?"

"Right here." Matt hurled himself toward them, so disheveled that Sunshine blinked. His dark blond hair was spiky as if he'd forgotten to brush it or had run his hands over it repeatedly.

Dark shadows made the green of his eyes brighter.

Her stomach clenched. She'd done that. Used her words to tear down the walls he'd built to insulate himself against his pain.

Dr. Turner gave him a terse nod. "Glad you could grace us with your presence."

Matt nodded curtly before his eyes darted to Sunshine. She glanced at the administrator before she caved to the urge to beg Matt's forgiveness for the harsh words of yesterday.

"Can we start?" Sunshine gestured to the open door behind Dr. Turner. "I have something else to do after this."

"Of course." Dr. Turner stepped back to allow her to precede him into the room.

She scanned the small space that had more framed certificates on the wall than an art museum had paintings.

When Matt pressed in behind her, she scurried to the chair furthest away from the door and angled it to face the administrator, not wanting to be too close to Matt. Or to smell that spicy clove scent she associated with him.

Dr. Turner's eyes darted between her and Matt. "Everything alright, you two?"

"Fine." She snapped the word off. She ignored his raised brow and rustled through her backpack for the slim folder containing her report of what they'd accomplished. She handed it to Dr. Turner, along with the updated flyer.

He accepted it and scanned through the sheets of paper. Sunshine sat on her hands, resisting the urge to gaze at Matt. Had her words pushed him further away from God?

Please, Lord, that's not what I want for him. I want him to know You for himself. To have a desire to spend time in Your presence—

"Everything appears to be in order." Dr. Turner gestured to

the papers in front of him.

"Yes, sir. The only thing left is to set up the venue."

Something they couldn't do until the day of the event. Not that there was much setup required. Sunshine had chosen activities that required few resources beyond the sand and the beach.

Dr. Turner nodded. "You've done an excellent job with this. Thank you." He cast his gaze between both of them. "I'll have people there to help you with the setup."

"Oh, I won't be here."

"You won't?" Matt spoke for the first time since he'd entered the room. "Why not?"

She cleared her throat. "My vacation was only through Boxing Day."

She planned to be on the first bus out of Orange Valley to make the long trip back to Portsville. After leaving her apartment locked up for two weeks, she'd need to clean it and get herself into the frame of mind for work the next day.

Matt touched the back of her hand, and she jolted. When had he gotten that close?

"I thought you were—"

She shook her head to cut off his words. This was not the place to have the conversation he was hinting at. Not with the administrator watching them with hawk eyes.

Matt buttoned his lips and jerked his head forward.

"Okay." Dr. Turner drummed his fingers against his desk. "We'll take that into account." He stood and extended a hand. "I won't keep you. Again, I'm grateful for all your help."

Sunshine shook his hand. "You're welcome, and good luck." She squeezed past Matt when he didn't move out of the way. Provoking man.

She clipped down the hall as if a colony of bats was after her. She hoped Dr. Turner delayed Matt long enough for her to get away.

"Sunshine."

"Really, God? You're determined to throw this man into my way, aren't You?"

Sunshine muttered under her breath, ignoring the nurse, who stared at her with concern. The poor woman was probably wondering if a patient had escaped from the psychiatric ward.

Then again, it could be because she was almost running away from Matt.

"Sunshine." His voice was closer than it had been last time. *Do not look back.*

That's how things always went badly in movies. The second the person looked behind them to check how close the other person was, they lost the race. Or got overtaken by the bad guy.

"Sunshine." A warm hand closed around her arm, and she conceded defeat, stopping in her tracks. She scowled at him. "What?"

She'd lost the race, but she didn't have to be gracious about it.

A gracious woman gains honor.

Her scowl deepened. Sometimes the proverbs she'd memorized were the bane of her existence. She sighed, turning to him.

"Why were you running from me?"

Great question, but one she didn't want to answer. She didn't want to explain how hard it was to be around him, with her harsh words playing on repeat in her mind. She went on the defensive.

"Well?" She tapped her foot. "You chased me all this way. What do you want?"

"Just to talk." Matt glanced around. The hall was no longer deserted. Doctors and nurses dawdled nearby, pretending disinterest in Matt and Sunshine's interaction.

Matt turned his glare on his colleagues. "Don't you people have any work to do? This is a hospital. Sick people need your help."

There were mutters, but everyone scurried away.

"Let's..." Matt held up a hand and ducked his head into the rooms closest to them. After the third room, he gestured to her. "Let's talk in here."

"I don't want to talk to you." She was as grumpy as he usually was.

"Please."

She exhaled and stalked into the room. "What's this about?"

Please, Lord. She didn't want to be responsible for any more broken lives.

"You were right."

Her eyebrows shot up. Not what she'd expected him to say. "About what?"

"I chose to turn my back on God rather than lean on Him after my parents' deaths."

Was this the answer to her prayers? Matt gave her a quick rundown of his conversation with his grandfather.

"I could use my grandfather as an excuse. He made it hard to be a Christian because of his pain and hurt over my grandmother's death, but—" He swiped a hand over his hair. "At what point do I stop blaming my grandfather for my choices and take responsibility for them?"

Was that what she was doing? Blaming her mother for

encouraging her to take a positive outlook on life? It was ridiculous when she put it that way.

She cleared her throat. "I don't know."

The corner of Matt's mouth quirked. "That's what I love about you. You always tell me the truth."

More like bludgeoned him over the head.

"Sunshine—"

"Elena."

His brows knit together. "What?"

"My name's Elena. Elena Fairchild." She wasn't sure if she ever wanted to be called Sunshine again. That name demanded its owner be optimistic and cheerful. After her mother's confession, she wasn't sure she could be that person anymore.

"You'll always be Sunshine to me."

"No." She dragged her fingers through her hair. "Sunshine is a woman who's always optimistic and upbeat. She sees the glass as half-full and is glad for the silver lining in the clouds."

"Isn't that you?" He brushed the sleeve of her turtleneck. "I can never see the color yellow without thinking of you."

He thought about her? She shook her head. Whether Matt thought about her was of no consequence.

"I'm not sure that woman ever existed." Tears clogged her throat as she remembered her mother's confession. "All this time, I assumed I'd inherited my sunny nature from my mother. Only to find out she'd been playing a role."

She told him what she'd learned the previous day.

"You're proving my point."

She gawked at him. "Did you hear anything I said?"

"Uh-huh." He nodded. "Everything. Your mother helped you through your grief the best way she could. But it was you, Sunshine," he clutched her hands in his.

"It was you who chose joy every single day. It was you who remained cheerful when faced with opposition or grumpy doctors who didn't know how to smile."

Was he right?

"You chose to become the woman you are—one who induces joy in everyone around her."

Her eyes filled with tears.

"Please don't cry," Matt almost growled. "I don't think I'm strong enough to withstand your tears. Not without kissing them away."

Sunshine's lips parted in surprise. Had he just said what she thought he had?

"Come with me." Matt lugged her out of the room. "I want to show you something."

* * *

Matt pulled Sunshine along behind him. He must be losing his mind. Why else would he tell Sunshine he wanted to kiss her? It was true, but why had he shared that tidbit with her?

He stopped outside John Ennis' room. "What I'll show you wouldn't have happened without you. Well, you and God."

He entered the room, trusting her to follow. Matt stood beside John's bed and checked the monitors. Everything was good.

"John?"

After a moment, the man's eyes fluttered open. Sunshine gasped.

"Doctor?" John blinked at him. "Don't tell me you're back to prod at me already."

"No." He rested a hand at the base of Sunshine's back and

pressed her closer. "I wanted you to meet Sunshine. She's the woman who prayed for you."

John's eyes shone with tears. "Thank you, Miss. Dr. Beckett told me they'd given up on finding out what was wrong until your prayer."

Sunshine clasped John's outstretched hand. "How?"

"It's a miracle." Matt fixed his eyes on her face. Would she realize what God had accomplished through her? "I got the call last night. This man is proof that prayer works." The call had come in after he'd left his grandfather's house on his quest for answers.

Tears spilled down her cheeks. "Thank you." She swiped at her tears. "I owe you an apology for what I said the other day."

"No." Matt gripped her hand. "It was hard to hear, but it made me ask some hard questions." He swallowed. "All this time, I've been blaming God when I should have placed the blame where it lay—on the people who killed my parents."

Matt thought about his encounter with Sunshine that day as he got dressed that evening. Ian and Marie had invited him to Trixie's bachelorette party. This time around, he didn't object to being used to even out the numbers, so Sunshine wasn't alone. His only complaint was that she hadn't been the one who'd invited him.

He studied his reflection in the mirror, wincing at the ugly sweater—the one he'd driven to Idlewood to purchase. There was no way he'd get caught shopping for anything Christmassy in Orange Valley.

With his luck, someone would see him, and by the time he got to work tomorrow, it would be all over the hospital. He hauled his dark gray coat over it—just in case.

On the drive to Trixie's house, he figured out what he would say to Sunshine. Seeing Sunshine without the enthusiasm and optimism he associated with her had been scary. She'd reminded him of himself, and that hadn't been good, because who needed another grumpy person in the world?

No. What the world needed was more people like her. People who chose joy and happiness when things were hard. Maybe even *because* things were hard.

If he wanted to be around Sunshine for more personal reasons, he had no one to blame but himself.

Eleven

A Tapestry of Emotion

Sunshine placed the final container of food on the table and stood back. Marie hovered nearby. They'd arranged for Keith to take Trixie out and had spent several hours getting things ready.

They'd cooked a large pot of rice and peas, curried mutton, fried fish, and made a garden salad. There was sorrel in the fridge, along with cucumber-melon juice. Marie had brought a small fruit cake, which Sunshine looked forward to eating with vanilla ice cream.

"Do we have enough food?"

Marie bit her bottom lip as she studied the table.

Sunshine whipped her head to gawk at the woman. "Are you kidding?"

Marie snickered. "You're right."

"The only thing left for us to do," Sunshine gently turned Marie away from the overladen table, "is take a shower and get dressed."

"We should call the guys." Marie glanced over her shoulder at the table.

"After we get ready." The worst thing would be if the men showed up while they were in the shower.

Within half an hour, Sunshine and Marie were ready and had confirmed that Keith and Ian were on the way.

"You look lovely." Marie shot her a mischievous grin. "I'm sure Matt's going to love that dress on you."

"M-Matt?" Sunshine smoothed her palms down the sides of her peach dress.

"Oh." Marie frowned. "Ian didn't tell you?"

Sunshine shook her head. Why didn't Marie hurry and tell her before she fainted from lack of air?

"We invited Matt to even out the numbers." Marie held up a hand. "Don't hate us. We saw how you two were the other night, and we hoped…"

Sunshine drew in a lungful of air. "Yes?"

"That the two of you could be friends?" Marie laid a tentative hand on her arm. "Matt's one of our closest friends—he has been since we met at university. It's important to us that the two of you don't hate each other."

Sunshine nodded. She needed to use words, or her sister-in-law would believe she'd been dumbstruck. She cleared her throat.

"Okay."

She could be friends with Matt. Even if his comment about kissing her popped up in her mind way too often. He was the first man who'd piqued her interest in years, and he didn't believe in God. Such a pity because she wanted to find out what it was like to kiss Matt.

The knock startled her out of her stupefaction, and she went to open the door. Please don't let it be Matt. She wasn't ready to face him yet.

"Sunshine." Matt stared down at her, his green eyes pulsing with emotion.

"Matt." She swiped a hand down the side of her dress. His eyes followed the motion, and she winced. What was she doing? She wasn't trying to attract Matt's attention. Where was all the animosity she'd had for him before?

"This is for you." He thrust a small gift bag into her hand.

"Thanks." It was a candle with the words "Be the light" in cursive. Did he understand the spiritual implications of those words?

He gestured to the bag. "So you can always remember why you're Sunshine." He cleared his throat. "Isn't that what Jesus told His followers? Be the light?"

Her mouth dropped open. Had he mentioned Jesus to her?

"Are you flirting with my sister?" Ian stomped up the steps and mock-scowled at Matt.

Sunshine groaned. Ian had the worst timing. Because yeah, from anyone else, what Matt had said would have been a simple encouragement, but from him, it had been the equivalent of a guy telling her he was interested and asking for her number.

Matt scowled at Ian. "Your timing is as impeccable as ever."

Ian grinned. "So you *were* flirting with her."

Sunshine's cheeks warmed. Why had she ever believed siblings were fun?

She glared at Ian. "As much as I'd like to continue this *ridiculous* conversation, you both need to get inside if we're going to surprise my mom."

She peered behind them. At least they'd been smart enough

not to park in front of the house and divulge their secret. She stepped aside and beckoned them inside.

God, did Matt refer to Your Son? What does that mean?

She had no time to contemplate his meaning before her mother and Keith showed up.

Trixie's eyes filled when she took in the scene. "Didn't I tell you guys not to host a bachelorette party?"

"This isn't a party, Mom." Sunshine kissed her mother on the cheek. "It's a small family dinner where we may or may not end up playing a few games."

Marie rubbed her hands together. "Oh, there will be games."

Sunshine grinned at Marie. "If the games happen to be wedding-themed, it's because we have weddings on the brain."

"Aww." Trixie enfolded her in a hug. Sunshine closed her eyes and enjoyed her mom's lavender-scented embrace.

She'd almost missed this—would have missed it if she hadn't pushed past her feelings of being overlooked and accepted Marie and Ian's apology.

Was there something holding her back from truly considering her mother's request for her to take over The Fair Child?

What if there was something wonderful that would happen after the transference of ownership, but she missed it because she was determined to hold on to what she had in Portsville?

Lord, I need Your help. Please help me to see what my next step should be.

She stole a glance at Matt. What if the two of them were on the verge of something beautiful and she didn't pursue it because she was afraid?

But what if she sacrificed her career at Bella Flora to remain in Orange Valley, and things didn't work out between them? What then?

Being an adult was hard because there were so many things that could go wrong if you made the wrong choice.

Make it crystal clear, God, because my heart's fragile.

* * *

"Let the games begin." Ian thrust his hands into the air as soon as the last person had put down their fork.

"Uh, no." Sunshine stood and began clearing the table. "Let the men begin the cleanup because Marie and I spent all day cooking." She gave Ian a sweet smile. "Then the games can begin."

Matt shuffled to his feet to help with the cleanup. He hoped for a few moments alone with her to ask her if she liked the gift. He hadn't been able to gauge the mood before Ian had shown up and ruined it.

"Get out of here, little sis." Ian swatted Sunshine out of the kitchen before Matt got a word out.

"Whatever." Sunshine laughed and placed the dishes she was carrying in the sink before leaving the room.

Matt smothered a growl. His friend was ruining his every chance to speak with Sunshine. He tracked her exit with his eyes. She'd made him a fan of bright colors. At least on her. When he turned to put his dishes in the sink, both Ian and Keith were staring at him.

"What?" His cheeks warmed, advertising his embarrassment to all. He dumped the dishes on the counter.

Ian folded his arms across his chest and scowled at him. "What are your intentions toward my little sister?"

"Uhm." He ran a hand over his head. He didn't have an answer to the question. Sunshine had flipped his world upside down, and he was still dealing with the fallout.

"You know that girl's a Christian, right?" Keith gave him a pointed look. "With your stance on God, pursuing something with her won't be in either of your best interests."

"I'm no longer committed to my previous viewpoint on God."

Ian gaped at him. "All the time Marie and I have been telling you about God, all we had to do was throw a pretty girl your way?"

Matt winced. He'd treated his friends abominably when they'd tried to share their faith with him.

"It wasn't quite like that." He gave them the abbreviated version of Sunshine's prayer, her accusation, his conversation with his grandfather, and John's miraculous healing. "Everything seems to point to a Higher Power."

Keith clapped a hand on his shoulder. "Trixie was right. God used Sunshine to show you things He'd probably been trying to tell you for years."

Matt tilted his head. Would God do that? Orchestrate an intervention? For him? A man who'd blatantly claimed not to believe in Him? A man who'd turned his back on the faith of his parents?

Matt was more subdued as he joined the women for the commencement of the games. The women had taken the dining room chairs and arranged them in the living room.

Matt plunked down on the chair nearest to him. Imagine that—the God who created the universe cared about him?

Sunshine sat beside him. "Are you alright?"

"Yeah." He shook his head. "No. I'm not sure." He propped his elbows onto his knees and dropped his head into his hands.

"Matt?" Marie rested her hand on his arm. "What's going on?"

He lifted his head. Everyone was staring at him. He blew out a breath. Okay. If he'd had this minor meltdown at the hospital, his job would have been in jeopardy. But around these people? They cared about him.

"Sorry. I have to wrap my mind around the idea that a God who had enough power to create the world out of nothing," his mouth trembled. "Without using a ball of gas but by speaking things into existence, cares enough about me to…"

"To what?" Sunshine rested a hand on his.

He turned his hand to clasp hers. He wanted this—someone who saw past his growl and realized he wasn't as grumpy as he appeared. Someone to speak hard truths he didn't want to hear, but that was necessary for change.

"Send you to me."

She lowered her eyes. He shouldn't have put everything out there like that. His grip tightened on her. He didn't want to lose her.

You can't lose what you don't have.

He loosened his grip. Hadn't he pledged to make peace with God before he pursued Sunshine or anyone else? He tampered down his emotions and focused on the bigger picture—getting answers about who God was.

"You were right."

Her eyes drifted back to his. "About what?"

"I chose the wrong side. Instead of leaning on God in my pain, I allowed it to drive a wedge between us."

There wasn't much he could have done as a child, but as he'd grown older, there had been many opportunities to choose God. In every instance, he'd made the deliberate choice to turn away.

He wet his lips. Dare he be this vulnerable with these people?

His eyes darted around the room. If he couldn't trust his friends, who could he trust?

"Where do I go from here?"

Twelve

Bachelorette, Salvation, and Games

Matt's vulnerability thrust a dagger into Sunshine's heart. His determination to learn the truth was real. The pressure to say the right words built until her chest tightened, but no words came.

"How familiar are you with the Christmas story?" Keith grabbed a chair and placed it in front of Matt before sitting.

Matt glanced at Keith. "I've heard it. Never paid much attention to it before because it seemed implausible."

Keith flashed a grin before leaning forward, resting his forearms on his thighs. "That's because you weren't in the right frame of mind to accept the truth."

Matt nodded. "Maybe not."

Trixie placed a chair beside Keith and sat. "Would you like us to tell you the story?"

Matt's Adam's apple bobbed as he swallowed. "Please."

The others rearranged the chairs until they sat in a circle.

"Well," Trixie began, "God created two perfect people. They had one restriction—don't eat from the Tree of the Knowledge of Good and Evil. Sadly, they disobeyed, and sin entered the world."

Keith held his hand open, and Trixie slipped her hand into it. "But God had a plan."

Oh. Sunshine's heart sighed. How could she not one hundred percent approve of a man who made room for her mother the way Keith did?

Matt cleared his throat. "What kind of plan?"

"The plan of salvation." Ian's eyes brimmed with joy. "God sent His Son, Jesus, to die for humanity. Christ died for the sins of the world—even those who don't acknowledge Him."

Sunshine winced. Did Ian have to be so blunt? But wasn't that what she'd done the other day in the park? And she'd done it without an invitation.

"Why?" Matt shook his head. "Why would Jesus need to die?"

"When humanity sinned," Sunshine joined the conversation. "All of us deserved death. Salvation was only possible if a perfect Person died on our behalf."

Marie laughed. "Put it this way, Matt. Let's say you'd read the procedure for performing a tonsillectomy. You'd watched videos and gone over the steps a thousand times in your head.

"Then the first day you started working at the hospital, they asked you to scrub in and perform the surgery on your own. Could you do that surgery without making a mistake?"

Matt groaned. "You know I couldn't. I told you what happened in my first tonsillectomy."

Marie grinned. "That's why I used that example."

Ian chuckled. Sunshine glared at them. "Okay. You guys can't have a secret inside joke and not share."

Matt turned to her. "The first time I did a tonsillectomy, I didn't cut the entire tonsil out."

She frowned. "Is that bad?"

"Extremely. Tonsils can grow back, often with the same issue as before."

"Oh."

"Luckily, the attending surgeon checked to make sure I'd done everything right. Otherwise," he shrugged, "I wouldn't be Doctor Grump."

"Us trying to live a perfect life without Jesus," Ian pointed at Matt, "is like you doing surgery on your own with only basic instruction." He shrugged. "Kind of."

Matt nodded. "I get it. Jesus died for us because He was perfect and we are not."

"Exactly." Trixie beamed at him. "It's His gift to us."

"How do I access that gift?"

Keith met Matt's gaze. "It starts by recognizing that you can't do it on your own. Accept that God exists, Jesus is His Son, and He came to earth to die for your sins. Can you do that?"

"Yes." Matt nodded. "I believe God exists, and that Jesus is His Son." His voice grew husky. "I no longer believe I can do this on my own."

Goosebumps pebbled Sunshine's skin. Was this truly happening?

God, is this You working in Matt's heart?

"That's it?" Matt's head swiveled to look at each of them.

Keith chuckled. "Not quite. Now you confess your sins, repent of them, and invite Jesus into your heart. Is that what you want to do?"

Matt's grip tightened on hers. "Yes."

Keith led Matt into a brief prayer of repentance. Sunshine

was in shock. And awe. She believed in the power of the Holy Spirit to transform lives, but what were the odds that God would use the event she'd feared would crush Matt to build him up?

After the prayer, Matt half-smiled at Trixie. "Sorry for ruining your bachelorette party."

Trixie beamed. "Are you kidding? Anyone can have a bachelorette party, but a party turned into a Bible study? Who does that? I'll be telling this story for years."

* * *

After Keith prayed for him and he accepted Jesus into his heart, Matt had expected to feel different.

Wasn't there supposed to be a supernatural change in his life? Wasn't he supposed to be filled with the peace, joy, and hope Sunshine had claimed God gave to those who believed in Him?

Sunshine's words floated back to him.

God isn't a circus monkey, Matt. He's capable of doing things we can't even imagine. And sometimes He does them, but He does everything in His timing and according to His will.

This must be one of those times when you wait. Matt settled back into the chair. Guess he should get comfortable waiting.

"Aren't there supposed to be games?" He pointed to himself. "If I went out and bought an ugly sweater for tonight, there had better be games."

Sunshine and Marie exchanged grins.

"Alright," Sunshine pulled away from him and stood. "You heard Doctor Glum. Let the games begin."

In short order, they rearranged the chairs. Again. Why had he ever thought it better to wall himself off from everyone?

This family had opened their door to him and quite literally changed his life.

Matt refocused his attention on Sunshine, who'd moved to stand in front of the row of chairs.

"Alright gentlemen, Mom, we're going to play Wedding Dress."

Matt groaned along with Keith and Ian, though he had no clue how to play the game. Marie lugged a case of tissue beside Sunshine, and he got a glimmer of their idea.

"No." His eyes dropped to the tissues, then flicked back to Marie.

Marie winked at him. "We figure six rolls of tissue should be enough for each of you to design a wedding dress."

Sunshine dolled out tissues, barely keeping her grin in check.

"What's the prize?" Ian cracked his knuckles. "There better be a prize."

"Bragging rights." Sunshine took her place beside Marie. "Everyone has ten minutes to come up with a design and create the dress. To show you how nice we are, you can use the internet."

"That's not nice," Keith grumbled. "This is you taking advantage of an elderly couple."

Ian snickered. "Nice try, Dad."

Keith designed a website for his consulting business after teaching himself how to do it and had an active social media presence.

Keith shrugged. "It was worth a try."

Sunshine returned to her seat beside him. "I'm with you."

"Yeah?" His grin slipped free.

Sunshine blinked at him. "That's the first time I've ever seen you smile. I like it."

They might not win the contest, but he'd have an excellent time draping Sunshine in tissue paper.

"Did you have any ideas for a design?"

Matt arched an eyebrow. "Don't tell me the wedding florist is out of ideas?"

"Your smile may have bedazzled me for a second." She dropped her gaze and began removing the wrappers from the tissues.

"Yeah?" He'd been mistaken about not being changed by accepting Christ. He'd never had this giddiness before.

"Hey," an empty tissue roll bounced off the side of his head. "Stop flirting with my sister and get to work."

Sunshine looked at Trixie and Keith with a beseeching expression. "Although the wedding's not for a couple of days, can we please give Ian up for adoption? We can keep Marie. I like her."

"I was planning to go easy on you, little sister, but not anymore. Get ready to crown me Tissue Paper Wedding Dress Champion."

Sunshine giggled. She didn't understand that Ian had thrown a gauntlet. Matt narrowed his eyes at Ian. "Challenge accepted."

He led her away from the others so they'd have privacy as they concocted their winning design.

They wasted the first two minutes searching for an idea on the internet before deciding to improvise.

"You could do an off-the-shoulder thing." Sunshine showed him what she meant. "Hurry." She glanced over to Keith and Trixie, who'd already begun their design.

"Alright." Matt began draping tissue over Sunshine's dress. "How do you always smell like a garden?"

A scent he was growing used to, and one he found intoxicating.

"I think it's all in your head."

"No. It's all you." Matt's hands shook as he wrapped the tissue around Sunshine's torso and down her legs. He wasn't ready for this. Tissue paper or not, Sunshine, dressed in white, made him fantasize about weddings and her walking down the aisle toward him.

Thirteen

Twinkle Lights and Dancing

Sunshine had given her mother time off to pamper herself in anticipation of her big day. Her major project for the day was wedding flowers. She'd start with her mother's bouquet, saving the smaller pieces for when her energy waned.

She collected her tools and the array of flowers she'd selected. She'd gone tropical, using the bold colors of the flowers to mimic her mother's personality.

Her cell phone rang as she snipped the end of the first bloom. She snatched it from the counter. "The Fair Child, how may I help?"

"Sunshine? Is that you?" The soft drawl jolted her.

"Angela?" Why was her boss calling?

"Why are you answering the phone that way? Please don't tell me my best florist is moonlighting with another agency?"

Sunshine rolled her eyes. "No."

Angela's paranoia about her staff leaving to work for the competition was legendary. It was one reason the compensation package for Bella Flora employees was so attractive.

"Did you forget? My family owns a flower shop. I've been helping my mother in between wedding stuff." And fundraiser planning, but Angela didn't need that detail. "What's up?"

Angela twittered, the sound putting Sunshine on edge. Her boss was in full "butter them up" mode.

Please don't let this be a case where she wanted Sunshine to return from her leave early. It had happened before—not that it was an option this time.

"Have I ever told you what a valuable resource you are?"

Sunshine groaned. "Angela, my mother's getting married tomorrow. I'm in the middle of creating her bouquet. I can't end my vacation early."

Nor did she want to. She had a surprising reluctance to leave Orange Valley now that the biggest obstacle between her and Matt had been removed.

"Of course not." Angela's chuckle held a touch of hysteria.

"Then what is it?" Guessing put her on edge. "Whatever it is, say it."

"Okay."

Angela drew in an audible breath, and Sunshine braced herself for the bad news.

"Nadia Barrett has hired us to plan her wedding. She wants *you* to do her flowers. She asked for you by name."

Sunshine's mouth dropped open. "Nadia Barrett knows my name?"

Nadia Barrett had made Saturn Island history twice. First, when she'd won a singing competition in Idlewood and gotten a gospel music contract. And then when she'd won the heart of R&B singer turned gospel artist Derek "JD" Walker.

"Yes, and there will be a lovely bonus for you."

It would be a boost for her portfolio. Sunshine's mind overflowed with possibilities. If she did the flowers for Nadia's and Derek's wedding, she would have so many bragging rights.

"We meet with her on the first Monday in January, as she's eager to get started."

"When's the wedding?"

"In June."

Depending on what was on the calendar for her when she got back to Portsville, six months wouldn't be a lot of time. Not to plan the wedding for two well-known artists.

"Well, I'll let you get back to it. See you in a couple of days."

The second Angela hung up, Sunshine put down the phone and did a happy dance. Nadia Barrett wanted Sunshine to do her wedding flowers and had asked for her by name.

"Eek!"

She did a fast jig, waving her arms over her head in excitement. She was doing the flowers for JD and Nadia's wedding.

"Is this some form of ritual?"

Sunshine whirled at the amused voice. "Matt. What are you doing here?"

She smoothed a hand over her messy bun. Why did he have to come into the shop when she wore her loose-fitting uniform? The one she'd had on yesterday was much more flattering.

She frowned. "Isn't the hospital in the opposite direction?"

Why did he decide to drop by and catch her in the most embarrassing moment of the day?

"Alright, fine. You got me." His green eyes met hers. "I wanted to see you. I came to ask if you'd have lunch with me."

"Matt." This wouldn't be a simple lunch. Why couldn't he

have come in a few minutes ago? Before Angela's call.

Because as much as she wanted to explore this thing between her and Matt, it wouldn't be fair to any of them.

"Matt, I'm leaving in a few days."

The corners of his mouth tightened. "I thought you were considering moving to Orange Valley."

"I was." She blew out a breath. She'd contemplated it while panicking about leaving her career behind. The call from Angela was a sign that her future was in Portsville, wasn't it? "My boss called. Nadia Barrett wants me to do the flowers for her wedding."

He frowned. "Who?"

Had he been living under a rock?

"You don't know who that is?"

Matt shook his head. Maybe he wouldn't. She didn't exactly sing the type of songs he'd have been interested in before last night.

"She's marrying JD Walker."

"Oh." Recognition flashed in his eyes. "That's a big deal for you, isn't it?"

She nodded until she felt like a bobblehead doll. "Huge."

"Buses run between Orange Valley and Portsville. So do flights. I drive, and Portsville is only about three hours away." The corner of his mouth quirked and Sunshine had the strongest urge to lean over and press her lips against his.

"Matt." She wanted to bask in the expression in his eyes. The one that made her feel beautiful and special. Wanted.

"Sunshine." Matt took her hands in his. "This isn't a marriage proposal. I'm inviting you to have a bite to eat and some conversation." His lips tipped up. "I'm sure you'll find new ways to call me Doctor Grump."

When he put it like that, it seemed simple.

"I can't." She gestured to the flowers. "I need to make these up." Since she was working alone, it would take longer than normal.

"Okay." He stepped back, and it was as if a wall had sprung up between them. "I get it." He tucked his hands into his pockets. "I'll see you around. Good luck with your project if I don't speak with you again before you leave."

He pivoted.

No. If he left, she'd never see him again.

"Come to the rehearsal dinner with me tonight."

* * *

Matt slipped into the back of the church, where Trixie and Keith would get married the next day. Someone had decorated the aisles with brightly colored ribbons and flowers until it resembled a garden.

Trixie wore a simple white dress as she strolled down the aisle toward Keith, who couldn't take his eyes off his future bride.

Matt had never wanted to get married. He'd focused on his career for so long that he seldom dated. Okay, he never dated, and that had been fine. He'd been content with his single status until now. His eyes drifted to Sunshine, who, for once didn't have a spot of yellow in sight.

Instead, she wore a red dress that made him reconsider his earlier reservations about the color. How had he ever professed that the color red was too loud?

On her, the color was perfect—complementing her skin tone and making him think of cold winter nights with her tucked against him.

Sunshine stood at the altar as her mother and Keith rehearsed their vows. A pang of longing swept through him. He wanted that. With her. The rest of the rehearsal passed in a whirl of yearning.

Matt stood as Sunshine approached. His view of her at the altar had not done justice to the dress. It hugged her from shoulder to waist before swirling around her legs.

Sunshine smirked at him. "Cat got your tongue, Doctor Grouch?"

"You look," his eyes roamed from her hair, which she'd twisted into some kind of updo down to her sparkly shoes. He swallowed. "Lovely."

Beautiful. Amazing. There were many other adjectives he could use to describe her, and none of them would capture how breathtaking she was.

"Why, thank you." Her lips softened into a smile. "You look pretty good yourself."

Was it vain of him to want to bask in the warmth of her smile?

"We should go." She pointed over her shoulder. "Everyone else is already on their way to the venue."

"Let's not keep them waiting." He tucked her arm into the crook of his for the short walk to the conference hall. For one night, he would enjoy being with Sunshine.

Matt entered the conference hall with Sunshine and blinked. Someone may have gone a little overboard with the lights. Twinkle lights were everywhere. On the tables and along the walls. They were on the Christmas tree that shimmered from the stage, and on the roof. It was like being under the stars.

"I suppose we have you to thank for this?" He gestured to

the decor.

She chuckled. "Oh no, this is Mom's brainchild. I'm an innocent bystander."

The last time he'd been at that conference hall was for a dinner honoring his grandfather for his years of service to the community.

His chest tightened. He should call his grandfather. They hadn't spoken since their last dinner. It wasn't that they were the best communicators, but there had never been a wedge between them before. Not one of this nature.

His grip tightened on Sunshine's. She glanced up at him. "Are you alright?"

"Yeah." This wasn't the time to burden her with his problems.

"Matt." She stopped, oblivious to the people who had to go around them. "What is it?"

He sighed. Wasn't it this desire to keep everything locked in that had caused the problems between him and his grandfather in the first place?

"I was thinking about my grandfather. We haven't spoken since the night of the Christmas miracle."

She frowned. "You mean the night God healed John?"

He gave a sheepish grin. "Yes. That's how I've been referring to it in my head."

It had seemed fitting, considering he'd always claimed miracles resulted from an overactive imagination.

"Did you call him?"

He snorted. "This may surprise you, Sunshine, but neither my grandfather nor I are the 'talking-on-the-phone' type of people."

She rested a hand on his arm. "Are you the 'talking face-to-face' type of people? Cause the two of you need to have a heart-to-heart conversation now that you're calm."

"Maybe. It's just," Matt's gaze flickered around the room. "Isn't this where Jesus is supposed to come in with His supernatural help?"

"Have you asked Him? Jesus is a gentleman, Matt. He won't wrestle anything out of your hands. He wants you to trust Him enough to take your problems to Him, believing He will help you."

He could do that. He could ask for help because it was obvious he wouldn't resolve this issue on his own.

"Thank you." He slid his fingers down to hers. "But that's trouble for another day. Tonight is about Keith and Trixie." And convincing Sunshine to take a chance on him.

An hour into the proceedings, Matt grudgingly admitted he was enjoying himself.

Sunshine bumped his shoulder. "Are you having fun?"

"Some."

She chuckled. "Don't bowl us over with your enthusiasm."

He scooped up the last forkful of peppered steaks. "The food's delicious."

Ian glared at him from across the table. "Are you sure it isn't because you're flirting with my sister?"

"No," Matt tilted his head and pretended to think. "Pretty sure it's the food, or because I'm the official Tissue Paper Wedding Dress Champion."

"You did not win." Ian jabbed a finger at him. "Our dress was way better than yours."

Marie and Sunshine rolled their eyes.

"Guys," Marie held up a hand. "Can we please not do this again?"

"Especially not in public." Sunshine giggled.

Matt glanced around. The people closest to them were staring.

"This is my fault." Marie shook her head. "I should have remembered how competitive you guys were and chosen another game."

"We're not competitive." He and Ian spoke at the same time.

"Right." Sunshine snickered. "What we should have done was get someone impartial to judge the designs."

"Or put them up on social media to get public feedback," Marie agreed.

"You're jealous because my date is prettier than yours." Ian winked at Sunshine. "And," he stood and extended his hand to his wife. "She's the better dancer."

Marie laughed and allowed Ian to pull her onto the dance floor, where a few couples were dancing.

Sunshine glared at them. "He doesn't know that. He's never seen me dance."

Matt smiled at her. She was breathtaking. Ian had given him the perfect excuse to have Sunshine in his arms. He'd be a fool not to take it.

"Would you like to dance?"

Fourteen

Moonlight Kisses

Sunshine slid her hand into Matt's and allowed him to lead her onto the dance floor. He slid his arm around her waist, drawing her closer to him. Oh, my, who knew a doctor had moves like this? It wouldn't do to get swept off her feet. She cleared her throat.

"I wouldn't have expected the man who hates Christmas to be so light on his feet."

"Dancing has nothing to do with Christmas. It's a valuable skill every man should learn."

"Oh?" She arched a brow. "Do you have many opportunities to use this skill?"

"I saved all my dance moves for you."

She tipped her head back to meet his gaze. "I bet you say that to all the girls."

His lips turned upward into a slight smile. She adored his smile.

"Do you want to get out of here?" He tipped his head toward the door.

"I thought you'd never ask."

Sunshine peeked at her mother before following Matt. "Where are we going?"

"You'll see." He glanced over his shoulder before pulling her through a door marked Employees Only.

"Should we be here?" Sunshine murmured as images of being kicked out during her mother's rehearsal dinner flashed through her mind.

"It's fine."

Matt coaxed her down a narrow corridor and up a flight of stairs. Her shoes clattered along the stairwell as she clambered after him.

"Matt." She was breathless by the time they got to the last step. Her cycling around town must not be effective, or it was the company.

"Look." Matt pushed open the door, and she gasped.

The full moon glowed with an otherworldly light. Stars twinkled against a midnight blue sky, so close she could almost reach out and touch them.

When was the last time she'd slowed down enough to notice the stars? God had created this world for her, and she was missing it.

"It's beautiful."

"Yes." He slid his hand against hers and led her to the edge of the roof. "From up here, everything is so peaceful." He sat and hung his legs off the edge.

"Uhm." She backed away.

He tilted his head to stare up at her. "Don't be afraid. I won't let anything happen to you."

"I don't want to ruin my dress."

Matt shucked off his jacket and spread it on the roof beside him. A slow smile spread across her face. Now she *had* to sit. The man would destroy a suit for her. She slipped off her heels and sat on the fabric, then swung her legs to dangle beside his.

"I'm changing your name to Doctor Daredevil."

"You're not in any real danger." He slid his arm around her.

Oh yes, she was. She was in danger of falling in love with him. And that was not the plan. She was leaving in three days.

"Do you come up here often?"

"Not recently."

"Oh-kay."

He sighed. "My grandfather was part of the citizen's association when I was growing up. They had a monthly meeting here. I loved the first part because there was always food, but the actual meeting was mind-numbing. I'd sneak up here until it was time to leave."

"How many other women had he taken up here?"

"You're the first."

Sunshine clapped a hand over her mouth. Had she said that out loud?

"And you'll be the last."

Dare she believe him? Being up here with him, with the city lights twinkling below, made it easy to forget about everything keeping them apart.

What would happen if she allowed herself to forget that they lived in different towns? That they'd only known each other for a short time?

He pulled away and turned to her. "I'm serious."

He cradled her face in his hands, and against her better judgment, she leaned into him.

"I've never felt drawn to a woman the way I am to you."

"I believe you." It was the same for her. Being with Matt made her dream of a different future, one where love and family were center stage. One that had her moving back to Orange Valley and taking over her family's flower shop.

But that would never do. If she walked away from the opportunity ahead, she'd always wonder if she'd made the right choice.

Hadn't she claimed she wouldn't worry about tomorrow? She kissed the palm of his hand. He hissed out a breath.

"Sunshine."

His low voice was gravelly, and for a second, Sunshine contemplated sliding her hands up to his head and pulling his mouth down to hers. Time to think about something else.

"What's your favorite memory of living in Orange Valley?"

There was a long beat of silence when she doubted he would answer.

"Well," he drew the word into two syllables. "There was this time I brought a girl up to the roof during a rehearsal dinner."

Sunshine bit back a smile and bumped him with her shoulder. "Come on, be serious."

* * *

Matt scrambled to get his thoughts in order. Sunshine's kiss had been a firebrand, and he was supposed to talk about his favorite memory? It was this moment, or any that included her. But she didn't want to hear that.

She'd already begun putting barricades between them.

Can you blame her? It's not as if you've shared that much about yourself.

That would have to change if he hoped to convince her they had a shot at being together.

"My favorite memory was probably the day my grandfather took me to the beach." He smiled at the recollection. "That may not seem significant since we live on an island, but Granddad worked all the time. And the one day he took off each week, he usually spent lolling around the house."

"How old were you?"

"About twelve." He'd been in high school and struggling to find his place.

"He had these goggles that he taught me to use and took me out to the reef. There were various types of fish and other sea creatures, but they all had a place on the reef."

Sunshine laid her hand over his. "Guess your grandfather noticed you were having trouble and wanted to remind you that you had a place."

He'd never considered that, yet it was a memory he'd treasured—one he'd drawn upon often to center him in uncomfortable situations.

Was it possible his grandfather had recognized his struggle and gifted him with the reminder that what he was going through was temporary?

"I never considered that."

"Your grandfather loves you."

"Maybe." He slipped his fingers between hers. "You won't stop until you've transformed me into a sunshiny version of myself, will you?"

The more time he spent around her, the less he resembled the grump everyone accused him of being.

She chuckled. "I was hoping your heart would grow to three times its normal size."

"You want me to have cardiomegaly?"

"Ha-ha. You know very well I'm not talking about your physical heart."

She rested a palm on his chest, and the organ in question galloped out of control. He shifted closer to her. Her unique floral scent drifted around them.

"I'm sure it's already grown bigger since I met you."

"That's nice." Her voice was breathy.

He caressed the curve of her ear, leaning in to whisper. "I'm fascinated by the way you smell."

"Oh?" She clutched at his shoulders.

"Hmm. I'd like to kiss you, Sunshine. May I?"

Please say yes. He couldn't go another minute without tasting her lips.

"Yes."

He slid his hand behind her head and kissed the pulse beneath her ear.

She gasped. "I hope that's not the only place you intend to put your lips."

"I'm working up to it." Now that he had her permission, he intended to take his time. He drew a line of tiny kisses from her ear to the side of her mouth.

"Matt," she slid her hands behind his head and drew him to her. "If you move any slower, it'll be morning before you reach my lips."

He grinned. "In a hurry, are you?"

"Yes." She pressed her lips to his.

Matt closed his eyes as sensations crashed through him. Sunshine was all light. Her sweetness made him want more. To become more.

He pulled away, chest heaving, but kept his hands on her.

"Sunshine, we should…" he swallowed hard. "Let's get back to the party."

His life would never be the same after that kiss. One taste of her lips had ruined him for anyone else. Since she was determined to leave, he'd have to figure out a way to live without her.

Fifteen

Chasing Happiness

She missed Matt, which was foolish. He'd told her he couldn't attend the wedding as he'd been scheduled to work on Christmas Eve months ago.

Maybe it was because, for one magical night, he'd pulled back the grumpy veneer he wore as armor and exposed the man she'd begun falling in love with. She groaned. She could not fall in love with Matt.

"Are you okay?" Marie cast her a concerned look.

"I'm fine." Sunshine stabbed the buttery fish fillet as if it were personally responsible for her upcoming heartbreak.

Marie's gaze flickered from her face to the fish she was flaying. "I'd hate to see what would happen to the poor fish if you weren't okay."

That was the trouble with being in the wedding party—sitting at the head table guaranteed that she'd be in the spotlight. She dropped the fork with a clunk.

"I'm going to…" she waved her hands, unable to come up with a suitable excuse before she rushed away from the table.

When tears pricked her eyes as she left the hall, she dashed them away with the heels of her hand. She would not cry over him. Not when she was the one orchestrating her own heartbreak.

Leaving is the best thing to do, right God? You wouldn't present me with such an amazing opportunity in Portsville only for it to be the wrong choice, would You?

She stalked out of the building and looked around without seeing a thing. Where was she going?

"Sunshine?" Marie's soft voice called as Marie and Ian caught up to her. "Are you alright?"

She rolled her eyes. "I'm not in the mood to have my head examined."

Marie's lips tightened.

"Sorry." Sunshine touched her sister-in-law's arm. "That was cruel. I didn't mean it."

"I understand." Marie's eyebrows drew together. "But we're not here in a professional capacity."

Ian stood at Marie's shoulder, united.

It must be nice to have someone at your side supporting you. Loving you.

Matt would love you that way. He would support you.

"Why are you here, then?" Her voice was harsher than she'd intended—because of her stupid inner voice.

"Did you forget what happened a couple of hours ago?" Ian pointed toward the church where Keith and Trixie had said their vows. "For better or for worse, you're stuck with me."

Sunshine groaned. "Are you sure we can't get a divorce?"

"Positive." His voice brimmed with amusement. "Ours is a

til death do us part kind of bond. And if I die before you, I plan to haunt you."

Sunshine chuckled at the ridiculous statement.

"Come." Marie took her arm and led her around the side of the building. "There's a gazebo where we can sit and talk."

Sunshine shook her head. "You guys won't let me go back inside until I tell you what's wrong, will you?"

"Nope." Ian's tone was cheerful as he fell in step on her other side.

The affection that built up in her chest was enough to push her sadness away. Almost.

A threefold cord is not quickly broken.

"Sit." Marie tugged her down to a wooden bench. "Tell us."

Sunshine mock-glared at Marie. "Is she always this bossy?"

"Yup." Ian sat beside his wife. "Is this about Matt? Did he hurt you?"

"No. Yes." She took a deep breath. "Yes, it's about Matt. No, he didn't hurt me."

Ian met her gaze with patience. "You know he would have been here if it had been possible, right?"

Her shoulders slumped. "Yeah. He's a fantastic guy." She smiled. He'd been so sweet last night.

Marie's grin was sly. "Are there wedding bells in your future?"

"No." She jerked at the image of herself walking down the aisle toward Matt. "Of course not. I'm leaving in two days."

Ian exchanged a look with his wife. "Trixie said you were taking over the flower shop."

"What?" Sunshine shook her head. She'd had no such conversation with her mother. It had surprised her that Trixie hadn't broached the topic again after suggesting they'd have to sell the shop.

Was this the reason? Had her mother assumed she'd take ownership of The Fair Child? Sunshine began making small laps around the gazebo. She couldn't—wouldn't—take over The Fair Child. It would ruin everything.

"Does Matt know you're leaving?" Marie stared at her in distress.

Sunshine nodded. "He does."

"Does Trixie know?" Ian's brows furrowed. "She and Dad leave for Europe on the twenty-seventh. Who's going to run The Fair Child?"

Why was this her problem? She'd made it clear that she had no desire to return to Orange Valley. Especially not now. Not when her career was on the verge of taking off to new heights.

"Well, it won't be me. I have a job at Bella Flora." She tilted her chin. "Nadia Barrett wants me to do her wedding flowers."

In the meantime, she'd have to come up with a plan to keep the shop open because the idea of letting her father's legacy die didn't sit well with her.

* * *

Matt drew in a deep breath before he knocked on his grandfather's door. The shift had been quiet, and he'd been thankful for the chance to work out what he wanted to say to his grandfather. Not that he'd made any significant progress, but he'd at least spent some time praying about it.

The door jerked open, and Alan Beckett glared at him.

"Come to accuse me of making more mistakes?"

"I—" Matt took a moment to examine his grandfather. They were of a similar height, though Alan's shoulders had rounded in recent years. He had a full head of hair, which had gone white along with his beard. Would Matt look like that if he lived long enough?

The reminder that life was fleeting prevented him from responding to his grandfather's snappy tone.

"Well?" Alan's scowl deepened.

"I came to apologize."

Alan gaped at him.

"May I come in?"

Alan stepped back for Matt to enter the house. It had been so long since he'd visited outside of their weekly dinners, that he wasn't sure where to go.

He tucked his hands into his pockets. "Can we talk?"

Alan grunted and headed toward the back of the house in silence. Alan entered his office and gestured to one of the two armchairs.

It had been years since he'd last been in this room. His grandfather's heavy desk no longer dominated the space. It had been pushed against a wall in the corner, and buried under piles of books.

What did his grandfather do all day? Matt stared at the man who'd raised him. Was it possible to spend your entire life around someone and have no clue who they were?

"Are you going to talk or stare at me all day?"

"I haven't been a good grandson to you, have I?"

The realization dawned on him that if Alan didn't insist on their weekly dinners, he'd probably never make the trip out here.

"What foolishness are you jabbering on about now?"

Matt gestured to the office-turned-library. "I have no idea what you do all day. Do you have friends? Do you leave the house?"

Alan snorted. "Of course, I leave the house. How do you suppose I get food to eat?"

Matt shrugged. Honestly, it wouldn't surprise him to learn that his grandfather used a delivery service. "We don't know each other well."

The truth saddened him. Two nights ago, he'd been angry at his grandfather for cutting him off from the church. But was it possible Alan had dealt with his grief the best way he could?

"Why didn't you want me to go to church after I moved in with you?"

Alan huffed out a breath. "Are we still on this topic?"

"Please," Matt kept his voice low. "The answer's important to me."

"I didn't have time to take you back and forth to church. I had a busy practice and a child to raise. I was fifty-five when your parents died. I had planned to retire at sixty.

"Lois and I were going to buy an RV and drive around Saturn Island. Then she died, and that dream died with her. A few months later, I became a single parent. I had to figure out how to do everything on my own."

His parents' deaths had had a greater impact than he'd realized.

"Why didn't you let the state raise me?"

Alan thumped his fists on the armrests. "No relative of mine is going to live in an orphanage. Not as long as there's breath in my body and I have something to say about it."

Huh. Matt leaned back in his chair. "I misjudged you. I believed you didn't want me here."

"Why would you believe such a stupid thing?"

The corner of Matt's mouth twitched. "I just did. We never went out, and there were days when you didn't speak to me."

"I was an old man who'd lost almost everyone in my family and was raising a child on my own." Alan pinched the bridge of his nose. "I should have done better, but without Lois," his shoulders lifted. "I'd lost my compass."

This was why Christ died for humanity. Because without Him, they had no direction. His grandfather had depended on his grandmother so much that when she died, he'd lost his way. But Alan had kept going because he'd had things to do.

Matt had trudged along in his grandfather's footsteps. First, because he'd been imitating his grandfather, and later, because it had become a habit.

"Can we start over?" Matt leaned toward his grandfather.

Alan arched a brow. "Do you plan to move back in and throw tantrums when you don't get what you want?"

"Was that a joke?"

"If you can't tell, we must not know each other as well as I thought." Alan stared down at his hands.

"We can change that. If you'd like." Matt swallowed. "Some friends invited me to have Christmas dinner with them. I'd like you to come with me."

He was certain none of his friends would object—not after they'd been so accommodating.

"Your friends wouldn't want you dragging along a curmudgeon of an old man. Go without me."

"No."

The urge to show his grandfather a glimpse into how family life could be was too strong to ignore.

Like him and Alan, the Wests and Fairchilds had experienced the death of a loved one. But rather than closing themselves off from love as the Becketts had done, they'd created new traditions. They had a culture of treasuring the family they had left. He wanted that for him and Alan.

Please, God, don't let it be too late for us to become the family You intended us to be.

"I won't go without you."

Alan narrowed his eyes. "Has anyone ever told you how stubborn you were?"

Matt bit back his grin. "It's a family trait—inherited from my grandfather."

"Hmph. I suppose they expect us to contribute to the meal. Why people spend hours in the kitchen cooking for one day, I'll never understand."

Matt spread his hands. "They asked me to bring a wrapped gift, but I'll take care of that. As for food, you could bring a dish. Or you can come with me and enjoy yourself."

Alan harrumphed. "What time is this dinner?"

Sixteen

Holiday Confessions

S unshine glanced at her mom. Trixie had been married less than twenty-four hours and glowed as if someone had turned on a flame inside her.

Sunshine, Trixie, and Marie were in the kitchen preparing the Christmas meal. Marie chopped carrots to add to the braised oxtail.

"This is so unfair."

Sunshine lowered the flame under the gungo rice and peas before responding to her sister-in-law. "What is?"

"That we have to be in this hot kitchen doing all the cooking while the men get to sit in the living room and watch TV."

Matt hadn't shown up, and Sunshine tried not to worry about what that meant. While she'd informed him of the plan, she hadn't given him a definite time to get there.

Instead, she focused on being present. She'd been careful not to define what was happening between her and Matt, telling herself it wasn't significant. If only she believed it.

Sunshine grinned at Marie's mock scowl. "True, but after dinner, they have the privilege of cleaning up our mess." She gestured to the sink that was already half-full. "Would you want to get stuck doing that?"

Marie grinned. "You have a point. Besides, we get to grill the most recent Mrs. about the joys of married life."

Marie cast a sly glance at her. "I'm hoping Trixie's stories will make you realize what you'll miss out on by not taking a chance on love."

As if she needed anyone to tell her.

Trixie blinked, her blissful expression changing to curiosity. Her mother's smile had been dreamy all morning.

"What are we talking about?" Trixie's gaze swung between Sunshine and Marie.

"Oh," Marie waved a hand. "I was trying to convince Sunshine to stay in Orange Valley."

Sunshine shook her head at Marie, but it was too late. Her mother's eyes narrowed at her.

"What does she mean? You're not staying in Orange Valley? Didn't we discuss this? I told you I planned to travel with Keith for his job."

This was not how she'd expected to have this conversation. Okay, so she wasn't exactly sure when she'd have had it since she was leaving the next day, but destroying Christmas had not been part of the plan.

Her gaze darted to Marie, whose expression had crumpled. Her sister-in-law mouthed an apology. Sunshine dipped her chin in acknowledgment before addressing her mother.

"We never discussed anything, Mom. *You* said I should take over the shop. I never agreed to it."

Trixie tilted her head. "Why would you want to work for someone else when you could be your own boss?"

Why would she want to be the boss? She'd been an employee her entire career and knew nothing about running a business. It had never occurred to her to take over The Fair Child. Besides, what if she failed, and they lost the shop because of her poor management skills?

"I-I can't."

Trixie shook her head. "I don't understand. Please explain it to me."

How did she explain something she didn't understand herself? Her mother wanted an answer that left no loose ends, but Trixie didn't realize that Sunshine's world had unraveled this Christmas.

The only thing that still made sense was the job she could do with her eyes closed. Well, not really because there were sharp, pointy things, but still...

"Sunshine's doing the flowers for JD Walker's wedding." Marie's bright voice was overly cheerful in the tense room.

Trixie frowned. "The R&B singer? You'd turn your back on your father's legacy to make flowers for a rhythm and blues singer?"

Her mother said the words as if JD Walker had leprosy or some incurable disease.

Sunshine cleared her throat. "He switched over to gospel. Remember?"

Trixie fluttered a hand. "Not the point. Your priorities are out of order, Sunshine. If you're going to chase after accolades and achievements rather than the more important things, you've made the wrong choice. I hope you figure it out before it's too late."

"I'm sorry." Trixie jerked off her apron and tossed it on the counter. "I can't do this now. I need some space to get into the right frame of mind, so I don't ruin what's left of Christmas." Trixie stalked out of the kitchen.

"I'm sorry." Marie enfolded Sunshine in a hug. "I forgot she didn't know."

"It's okay." It wasn't, but it made no sense for both of them to be unhappy. Sunshine choked down her tears and took a step back. "What did she mean by more important things?"

"Uhm," Marie bit the inside of her lip. "I'm not sure what Trixie meant, but," She met Sunshine's gaze. "I empathize with you. Pursuing your career is easier than chasing after love. With a job, there are certain things you can do that may lead to a particular result.

"Love's not like that. It's always a risk. It means putting yourself out there over and over again. Fear of getting hurt will prevent you from taking chances."

"This conversation wasn't about Matt. It was about the flower shop."

"Wasn't it?" Marie quirked a brow. "From where I'm standing, they're the same things. Both require a decision of the heart, which you refuse to make because you're afraid."

"I—" Was that true? Sunshine stared blindly around the room. She stumbled to the stove and tested the rice, snapping the flame off.

"Can you finish up? I need to get some fresh air."

She angled her head away from Marie, not waiting for confirmation before she sped out of the room. For the first time in her life, Sunshine wished she had a car.

If she'd had one, she'd have jumped into it and driven until she was back in Portsville—away from these decisions that all led to heartbreak.

* * *

Matt parked in front of Trixie's house. He'd finally convinced his grandfather that his friends expected them at the house in the morning. Alan had insisted they would not show up before breakfast—a concession Matt had grudgingly made.

If this was going to be his last day with Sunshine, he wanted to spend every second with her. Had it been up to him, he'd have been there at sunrise.

"Are you sure these people are okay with me being here?"

Matt got out of the car and grabbed the bag with the gifts from the back seat.

"I'm sure. Are you coming?"

Alan grunted and pulled himself out of the car. His grandfather was acting like a grumpy child. Sunshine's teasing names for him flashed through his mind, and he almost smiled.

"I'm going to call you Grumpy Gramps."

Alan glared at him. "You'll do no such thing." Alan stomped up the steps and stood before the wreathed door, hands in his pockets. "What kind of people have wreaths on their doors?"

Everyone except them.

"People who celebrate Christmas." Matt rapped on the door.

"Infernal holiday with too-cheerful music and bright colors."

The corner of Matt's mouth twitched. "You're enjoying this, aren't you?"

"Prove it."

The door opened, and he swung his attention forward. Sunshine wore a red apron with the words 'We whisk you a Merry Christmas' over her jeans and thick lemon-colored sweater. His lips twitched in response to the quip until he met her eyes.

"What's wrong?"

He held out the bag to his grandfather, stepping forward when Alan grabbed it.

She shook her head. "Nothing."

He cradled her face in his hands, angling it to peer into her eyes. "Liar. Someone hurt you."

Was it him? He wracked his mind for anything he could have done to cause her this level of sadness.

"Is it because I didn't come yesterday? I explained—"

"No." She placed a finger against his lips. "I'll explain later." Her eyes flickered behind him before she pulled away.

"Hello." She rubbed her palms against her apron. "You must be Alan Beckett." She extended a hand. "Nice to meet you, sir."

"The pleasure's all mine." Alan clasped Sunshine's hand, bending to peck the back of it.

Matt gaped at Alan. Who was this man?

"You didn't imagine I won your grandmother's heart by being Grumpy Gramps, did you?" Alan winked, teasing a smile from Sunshine.

"Let me show you where the men are hanging out." She raised an eyebrow. "Unless you want to help Marie in the kitchen. She's…" she cleared her throat. "Dinner's almost ready, but she's handling what's left by herself. Mom and I…" Her mouth tightened.

Ah. Whatever had happened between her and Trixie was the reason Sunshine had lost all her shine.

"I can help in the kitchen." Alan tucked Sunshine's arm into his and waggled his eyebrows. "That way I'm spared from the clean-up later on."

Sunshine chuckled, and Matt bit back a growl. His grandfather needed to find his own girl.

He followed them into the kitchen, where the aroma of well-seasoned meat and savory rice greeted him. Dinner was going to be delicious, but the tension that simmered in the air fueled his determination to get Sunshine alone to find out what was troubling her.

"Hey, Marie," he nodded at his friend. "I brought you a recruit. He's not acting like the man I grew up with, so be on your guard. Aliens may have taken over his body."

He towed Sunshine away from Alan and through the door. He didn't stop until he was outside on the veranda and had settled her on one of the long wicker chairs.

"Now," he clasped her hands in his. "Tell me what happened."

She stared at their hands. Did the variance in their skin tones fascinate her as much as it did him? If they had children, whose complexion would they inherit? The dark brown of their mother's or his lighter one?

He shook his head. Now was not the time to get distracted by a dream that would never come true.

She wet her lips. "It's nothing."

He tipped her chin up. "It's not nothing. Talk to me. Please."

She sighed, the action lifting her shoulders and chest. "My mom found out today that I won't be staying in Orange Valley?"

He frowned. "Didn't she know that?"

His heart had started an hourly countdown clock the second she'd told him she was leaving. It was less than twenty-three hours before her bus left Orange Valley.

"Guess not. Turns out the two of us were living under different assumptions."

He chafed her hands in his. "She was upset."

Sunshine's eyes filled. "I ruined Christmas, Matt."

"Pretty sure it's impossible to do that. The devil has more power than you. He tried and failed."

Sunshine's pretty brown eyes widened. "What? How?"

He grinned. "I may have been reading the book of Luke."

He'd been intrigued because Luke had been a doctor. He'd kept reading because Luke's account of Jesus's life was a simple, yet detailed presentation of the facts that allowed the reader to analyze and draw his own conclusions.

She smiled. "That's great, Matt. I'm glad you accepted Jesus into your life this holiday."

"Are you sure you're letting Him have full control of *your* life?"

The words popped out of his mouth almost without his permission.

Sunshine's mouth dropped open. "What did you say?"

He swiped a hand over his face. "I'm sorry. The words seemed to have a life of their own. Ignore me. But I'll give you some advice I received from a wise woman.

"Have you asked Jesus to help you make the right decision? He wants you to trust Him enough to take your problems to Him, believing He will help you."

Her eyes softened. "You think I'm wise?"

He met her gaze, allowing himself a few moments to get lost in their caramel depths. "I believe you're many things. Beautiful. Intelligent. Caring. I love the way you see people and walk with them when they're going through a hard patch."

How had he ever considered that a character flaw?

"I love the way you push people to be better. The way you light up a room. I love…"

You. He loved Sunshine. Somewhere between planning the

fundraiser with her and spending time with her family, he'd fallen in love with her.

Tell her.

How was he supposed to survive her return to Portsville? Because when she left, she'd take his heart with her.

Tell her you love her.

How was he supposed to confess his feelings for her when she'd made it clear she had no intention of staying?

He'd move. He could get a job in a hospital in Portsville. His grandfather would understand, wouldn't he?

Tell her.

"You love…?" Sunshine's tongue darted out to wet her lips. His eyes followed the motion, momentarily distracted. "What else do you love about me?"

Tell her you love her or lose her forever.

"Everything. I love everything about you. Sunshine, I love you. I'm so in love with you I don't know how I'm going to survive when you leave."

Seventeen

If Wishes Were Horses

"Matt." Her heart stuttered.

"Shh," he put a finger to her lips. "My timing sucks, but I had to tell you how I felt."

His Adam's apple bobbed. "I wish…"

His voice trailed off, and Sunshine filled in her desires. She wished Nadia Barrett had never contacted Angela. That she wanted to take over The Fair Child. That there was a way to do what she loved and remain in Orange Valley. She wished her and Matt's love story was an easy one.

Most of all, she wished she didn't have to leave.

Matt rested his forehead against hers. "We can have a long-distance relationship."

"Maybe." Her heart ached because it was futile. Between his schedule and hers, they'd never see each other.

Why was this so hard? Why couldn't this be one of those Christmas romance movies? She and Matt would fall in love, and life would magically work itself out.

"Hey." Matt pulled away from her and cradled her face in his hands. She liked it when he did that. "Go. Patch things up with your mom."

"I will." But first, a kiss.

She closed the distance between them and kissed him. If she was going to leave her heart in Orange Valley, she'd at least have a few more of Matt's kisses to keep her warm at night.

He changed the angle of the kiss, and it was like sliding into bliss. Matt's kiss was everything she loved about Christmas. It was sweet and passionate, with enough heat to make her forget the cold.

The kiss ended long before she was ready.

"Go." He pulled away, his chest heaving. "The longer you stay here, the harder it's going to be for me to allow you to leave."

She scrambled to her feet and hurried into the house. Being with Matt made her question everything. Was she making the right choice? Could she start over in Orange Valley? Did a long-distance relationship have any hope of working, or was she fooling herself?

Sunshine stood outside her mother's room, Matt's words echoing in her head.

I love everything about you. I'm so in love with you I don't know how I'm going to survive when you leave.

For someone who sought to choose joy in every situation, she'd sure made a mess of things. She'd hurt her sister-in-law. Her mom was mad at her and she'd broken Matt's heart. The man had confessed his love for her, and she'd said nothing.

She rested her palm against her mother's door. Well, she'd kissed him, which only made everything more confusing.

She knocked, entering at her mother's response. She closed

the door and rested her back against it, inhaling a lungful of lavender-scented air.

"Mom."

Trixie had kicked off her shoes and crawled into the center of the bed. How many times had Sunshine clambered into bed beside her mom? Trixie always knew the right things to say to pull her out of her mood.

The last lingering bit of resentment for her mother's choice to mourn her father in private melted away. Thanks to her mom, she'd grown up knowing her parents loved her.

Her mother had created a safe space for Sunshine, a place she could retreat to when hurt or in pain. A place where there was always an abundance of love.

"Mom." Her voice broke when Trixie met her gaze.

Trixie sat up, her forehead scrunched. "What is it, sweetie?"

Sunshine scrambled over to the bed and crawled into Trixie's arms before the first tear fell.

"Oh, come now," Trixie soothed, running her hands over Sunshine's back. "There's no crying on Christmas Day."

"I've ruined everything."

She'd said something similar to Matt. She should change her name from Sunshine and call herself something more fitting, like Devastation or Destruction. Carnage. That would be a cool supervillain name.

She'd swap out all the yellow in her wardrobe with gray— gunmetal gray. The image was so ridiculous that her tears stopped.

"Good." Trixie peered at her. "You know there's nothing you can do to make me stop loving you, right?"

Sunshine bit her lip. "Even if I walk away from The Fair Child?"

"Oh honey," Trixie's sigh came from the depths of her soul. "I've been thinking about that since I came up here. Until this Christmas, I don't believe I ever told you The Fair Child was your legacy.

"I've always encouraged you to follow your dream. You were so passionate about flowers that I assumed you'd want to take over from me someday."

The tension in Sunshine's shoulders eased a bit.

"You're not mad at me because I'm returning to Portsville?"

"I'm disappointed you won't remain in Orange Valley, but that's hypocritical, isn't it? Pressuring you to stay while making plans to leave." Trixie hugged her. "We'll figure this out."

"What about the deliveries you have scheduled?"

As a florist, she understood the importance of getting the flowers you ordered on time.

"I'll make a list. You, Ian, and Marie can take turns handling them until Keith and I get back."

Was it that simple? Could they resolve problems with a bit of compromise?

"Is there anything else bothering you?"

Hadn't she said enough? On what should have been the first day of Trixie's honeymoon, she'd started a fight almost as epic as some they'd had when she'd been a teenager.

She shook her head. This day couldn't handle any more drama.

"Are you sure?" Trixie's lips curved into a teasing smile. "You don't have something to tell me about you and a handsome blond doctor with smoldering green eyes?"

She mock-glared at her mother. "Didn't you get married yesterday?"

Trixie chuckled. "I love Keith with all my heart, but he's no

Doctor Grump."

No. He was not. Sunshine wasn't sure if there was any other man comparable to Matt. Not as far as she was concerned.

"Is love worth it?"

Trixie's expression softened. "Absolutely. But that's a decision you have to make for yourself. Especially if you have to choose between two desirable things. You must determine what you're willing to leave behind."

* * *

This was the first Christmas Matt would celebrate in more years than he could remember. After he'd convinced Sunshine to speak with her mom, he joined Ian and Keith in the living room.

"We're watching Die Hard," Ian winked at him, "before the women come in and force us to watch some sappy Hallmark movie."

He settled on the two-seater couch, feigning interest in the movie while his heart was upstairs with Sunshine and Trixie.

Was everything okay? Should he ask God for help? He wasn't sure. But if the things that mattered to him were important to God, he should pray.

Please, God, let everything be alright between Trixie and Sunshine. And if it's not too much trouble, can You work things out between me and Sunshine, too?

Five minutes later, Marie and his grandfather joined the group.

"What are you guys watching?" Marie stared at the television screen.

Ian waggled his eyebrows. "The best Christmas movie of all

time."

"Right." Marie rolled her eyes and perched on the arm of the chair Ian was sitting in.

Alan settled into the other armchair. Marie glanced around the room. "Where are Sunshine and Trixie?"

Matt pointed to the roof. "Upstairs."

Marie's brow furrowed. "Is everything okay?"

Ian paused the movie and frowned. "Did something happen?"

Marie rested a hand on Ian's shoulder. "Trixie found out Sunshine's not staying."

"Oh, no." Ian's gaze flitted to the roof. "We should pray for them."

"Agreed." Keith stood and held out his hands.

Marie and Ian joined hands, waiting until Matt and Alan joined them.

"Father," Keith began, "we place Sunshine and Trixie into Your hands. Help them understand each other's viewpoint without getting angry at each other. Lord, we know You have a plan. May Your will be done in this situation. Amen."

After everyone retook their seats, Alan met his gaze. "I understand why you like this group. If I'd had friends like this after—"

After Grandma Lois and his parents had died.

Alan cleared his throat. "We'd have been fine."

"We are fine," Matt spoke the words he wanted to be true.

"You know Die Hard isn't a Christmas movie, right?"

Matt's head swiveled to Sunshine, his eyes resting on hers. She nodded, and he exhaled.

"What?" Ian sputtered. "Of course it is. We may have to rethink our familial ties."

Sunshine slapped a hand to her chest. "You'd disown me over

a movie?"

"Now, children," Trixie smirked at the two of them. "No squabbling or we won't play any of the games I planned for today."

Both Sunshine and Ian pantomimed buttoning their lips in such perfect synchrony that it was as if they'd rehearsed it.

"Let's watch the rest of the movie." Trixie snuggled next to Keith on the sofa.

Matt stretched his arm along the back of the two-seater and inclined his head toward Sunshine. Would she come? To his delight, her lips curved into a soft smile as she made her way over to him.

The second she sat on the couch, he drew her closer to him. She sighed and snuggled against him. Matt breathed in Sunshine's floral scent. Best Christmas ever—if only it could last forever.

Eighteen

Elephants, Candy Canes, and Complications

Sunshine snuggled against Matt and inhaled deeply. She would buy a bottle of cloves when she returned to Portsville. Matt's arms enveloped her in warmth, his chest firm under her cheek.

Was she making a mistake by returning to Portsville? Or should she stay in Orange Valley and take over The Fair Child?

Because this thing between her and Matt felt right—as if it could last forever. But that was foolish, right? People didn't fall in love after a couple of weeks. All too soon, the credits were rolling.

Trixie jumped up and clapped her hands together. "Time for our Christmas White Elephant."

"What's that?"

Matt's low voice near her ear made her shiver.

"You'll find out. Forget everything you've ever heard about

the game. Mom never plays it the same way twice. One year we played it at church and she combined it with musical chairs." She grinned at the memory.

"Thanks for all your lovely contributions." Trixie gestured to the gifts under the tree like a television game show host. "Each participant will get to take home one of these fantastic items."

"Does she always talk like she's on a game show?" Matt murmured.

"No." Sunshine turned her full attention to Trixie. "That's new."

"There are thirty candy canes hidden in the yard. The person who brings back the most gets to select the first gift, and so on after that."

Matt's gaze flitted between her and Trixie. "Is she serious?"

"As a heart attack."

"Bring it on." Ian stood and shuffled like a boxer going into the ring.

"Everyone in this family has lost their mind." Alan's head swiveled to take in everyone. "I like it." Alan stood and rolled his neck.

Sunshine stared at Matt. "Didn't you say your grandfather was..." How should she put it? "Not fun."

Matt frowned at Alan. "I'm not sure what's going on. He wasn't like this when I was growing up."

"No?" She shifted to look at him. "What changed?"

"If I had to guess, I'd say he'd been Sunshined." Matt smoothed his hand over her cheeks.

"I never met the man before today. How am I responsible for the change in him?"

"You changed my life, and I rubbed off on him." Matt kissed her lightly.

"Less kissing, more candy cane finding." Alan winked at her. "If the boy had wanted to kiss you, he should've brought some mistletoe with him."

Everyone was staring at them. Sunshine's cheeks warmed. She'd forgotten where they were.

"Well," she pulled herself away from Matt. "What's everyone waiting for?"

Alan Beckett won the candy cane game. The man had an uncanny ability to ferret out where Trixie had hidden the red and white canes.

"You cheated." Sunshine threw an arm around Matt's grandfather.

"No, ma'am." He grinned at her. "Though I'll give you one of mine, so you're not too embarrassed to have been beaten by this old man." Alan handed her one of his candy canes.

She accepted it and kissed him on the cheek, ignoring the way his face reddened. She'd only found one candy cane. Matt had distracted her, making it hard for her to focus. It should be illegal for doctors to look like him.

She trailed into the house with everyone else, resigned to the reality that she'd be the last person to select a gift from under the tree. It didn't matter to her. Today was all about making memories. Her eyes slid to Matt.

Sunshine usually enjoyed playing games on Christmas Day. Not today. She wanted to fast-forward to the time after dinner when she and Matt could sneak away for a few minutes together.

By dinner time, she'd laughed so hard, she should have a six-pack. The gag gifts ranged from the resourceful to the ridiculous. The most ridiculous was the housecleaning shoes Ian had picked. The pink shoes he insisted on wearing even now.

Sunshine rolled her eyes at Ian. "You'll hurt yourself if you don't take those slippery things off."

"You're just jealous that I'm edging you out in Mom's heart as her favorite child."

Everyone froze, as a hush fell over the room.

"You called me Mom." Trixie shuffled over to Ian and lifted a trembling hand to his face.

"I know." Ian gave Trixie a sheepish look. "Is that okay?"

"It's perfect." Trixie pulled his head down to kiss him on the cheek. "I always wanted a son."

"Sunshine?" Ian came over to her and took her hands in his. "Is it okay if I call Trixie Mom?" His eyes searched hers.

Sunshine took a moment to examine her heart. There wasn't a shred of jealousy left. In the time she'd spent with Ian, she'd begun to think of him as a brother. Besides, the expression on her mother's face made it clear what Ian's declaration had meant to her.

"Of course, silly. Ours is a 'til death do us part' kind of relationship." She tapped his chin. "If you die before me, there may be some haunting."

They grinned at each other.

"What am I?" Keith stomped over to them. "Chopped liver?"

Sunshine rolled her eyes. "No, Dad, you're a grumpy old man."

Could she love Christmas more than she already did? She wouldn't have considered it possible before she came home, but now she did.

God had extended her family—He'd given her siblings, an earthly father, and a man who loved her. She was about to get a boost in her career, not to mention her finances.

It was more than she'd had at any other time in her life. So why did it feel as if things were spiraling out of her control?

* * *

"Does she know you're in love with her?"

Alan kept his gaze fixed on the windscreen as he asked the question.

"Yes." Matt parked in front of his grandfather's house. The plan was to drop Alan off and then zip back to Trixie's, to spend an hour or two with Sunshine before returning to the hospital.

"Will you be marrying her?"

"No."

Alan glared at him. "Why not?"

Matt huffed out a breath. "It's complicated."

Alan snorted. "You young people complicate everything. Love is the most natural thing in the world. If you love the girl and she loves you back, you ask her to be your wife. Then you get married and start your life together."

If only. His grandfather made it sound simple. He loved Sunshine, and he believed she had feelings for him too, but was it love?

"How would we spend time together? She lives in Portsville and I live here." And the shifts at the hospital were brutal. He'd never noticed how bad it was until Turner adjusted his schedule for him to help plan the fundraiser. Leaving while the sun was still in the sky on the same day his shift started had been nice.

Alan harrumphed. "What about going into private practice?"

"I thought about it." Since they were being honest, he may as well confess everything. "I also considered looking for a job in

Portsville, but…"

"But what?"

"You're here." He and Alan were finally acting like a family. He didn't want to lose contact with his last family member. "Besides, I like Orange Valley." It was a wonderful place to raise a family. If he ever had one.

"You have a lot to consider."

Matt plopped his head against the headrest. "If you were a praying man, I'd ask you to pray for us."

Alan grunted. "If you keep acting like a stubborn fool, I may have to start." He unbuckled his seatbelt. "Go get your girl, Matt, and don't be too proud to beg her to stay."

Could he do that? Could he ask Sunshine to stay in Orange Valley? Alan's words played in his head as he drove back to Trixie's house. No, he wouldn't ask her to give up her dream. It would be better for him to figure out a way they could work around their schedules and separate cities.

She waited for him outside. Sunshine sat on the swing, a red and black checkered blanket around her shoulders.

"Hey," he bounded up the stairs. "You were supposed to wait for me inside."

She wrinkled her nose. "Too crowded—everyone's staying for the night."

Did they subject her to the same third degree he'd received? It would have been worse for her, having to fend off questions from four people.

"How much time do you have?"

"About an hour."

"Let's not waste it. Come here." She opened her arms, making space for him under the blanket.

Matt wasted no time tucking her against him. She fit against him perfectly. She sighed, and Matt set the swing in motion. Though it was only after five, the sun had set and darkness crept over Orange Valley. As it did, twinkle lights popped up all over the community, including at the Fairchild's.

"If you could have one wish, what would it be?" Her voice was soft in the stillness.

Your love. I wish for a lifetime with you.

He refused to tell her that. The last thing he wanted to do was make her believe she had to choose between her career and him.

"Another day with you. I'd wish you could attend the fundraiser to see how your plan turned out."

"Hmm. That'd be nice."

"Are you sure you can't stay another day?" So much for his plan not to pressure her. "I'd take you home."

She turned her head to look at him. "You'd drive three hours to take me home and three hours back?"

He shrugged.

"Oh, Matt," she kissed his cheek. "Thank you, but no. I'd worry about you the whole time. Suppose you got into an accident, or they paged you while you were still hours away. It's better this way."

Not for him. He bit back his protests because, though he wanted her to be wrong, she wasn't.

"Okay." He stroked her cheeks. "In that case, I have another wish."

"Yeah?" Her tongue darted out to wet her lips, and his eyes dropped to track the motion. "What's that?" Her voice came out breathy.

"A kiss."

"Only one?" She scooted closer and swung her legs over his

lap.

"Hmm. One." He kissed her cheek, enjoying the way she shivered at his touch. "Or a thousand. I'm not sure how many kisses I can get in before it's time to go."

She locked her arms around his neck.

"Why don't we stop wasting time and start kissing?"

"Yes, ma'am." He lowered his head to hers. "Your kiss is my command."

Nineteen

Signs and Bittersweet Goodbyes

Sunshine tiptoed out of the house the next morning. Her bus didn't leave for hours, but she preferred to wait at the terminal rather than suffer through another painful goodbye.

Last night with Matt had been hard enough, though both of them had been careful to avoid the word.

She pulled the door closed behind her and crept down the steps, finding it harder while carrying her suitcase than she'd anticipated.

She hefted the case, nearly waddling under the weight as she approached the taxi she'd hired.

Tim opened the door at her approach and hurried toward her. "Sunshine."

"Shh." She glanced over her shoulder. His greeting had been way too loud in the early morning.

Tim lowered his voice. "Are you sneaking away?"

She grinned at his good-natured teasing. "You're my getaway driver."

He took the suitcase and carried it the rest of the way. Sunshine got in the backseat and ducked as he drove past her house. She didn't take an easy breath until he'd turned onto another street.

After Tim dropped her off at the terminal, she made a last-minute decision and pulled her suitcase to the restaurant across the street.

Sunshine claimed an empty table, and after placing an order for French toast and chocolate tea, pulled up the Bible app on her phone. She loved having access to the Word from anywhere in the world. A few taps, and she was in Proverbs.

By the time she'd finished her meal, she was halfway through the book. She savored the many nuggets of truth, but it was the concept of wisdom that lingered in her mind.

Was she being wise? Or doing what she wanted instead of following God's directions?

The fear of the LORD is the beginning of knowledge: but fools despise wisdom and instruction.

She didn't want to be a fool. The book of Proverbs made it clear the type of treatment fools deserved.

Lord, am I being foolish? I want to be a woman You can trust to carry out the assignments You've given me. Make it crystal clear if I'm doing the right thing by leaving. Please, Lord. Open my ears, eyes, and heart so I don't do the wrong thing.

She sat for a few moments with her eyes closed, hoping for something. Would God give her a sign? She'd asked Him to, and she believed He would, but would He answer?

"Are you okay, honey?" The buxom woman who'd served her meal studied her with concern.

"Yes," Sunshine's gaze dipped to the name tag clipped to the woman's powder-blue uniform. "Becky. I'm fine. Thanks for asking."

"Alright honey, just wanted to make sure. Are you about ready?"

Sunshine's gaze flitted around the room, which had filled up since she'd gotten there. She checked the time. Her bus would pull into the station any second.

"Yes."

Becky handed her the bill. "Did you enjoy your breakfast?"

"Yes, thank you. It was delicious."

She paid and pushed her chair back.

"Would you like to buy a ticket to a fundraiser we're having today at Sapphire Beach?"

Sunshine blinked. "I didn't know they were selling tickets here."

And in all the planning, that was the one thing she hadn't done—bought a ticket.

"Oh, honey, they're not." Becky waved a hand. "But when I found out the proceeds were for medical bills, I bought a few of them and got permission to sell them at work. I've done that several times already."

Becky winked at her. "What do you say? Can I entice you to support a charity?"

She handed over the money and collected her ticket.

"I can do this." Sunshine trudged toward the terminal. "I have a terrific job and a fantastic apartment. In a few weeks, I'll meet Nadia and Derek."

There was a bit of a fan girl peeking out, even as a part of her wanted to return to her childhood home. She handed the bus driver her bag, which he stowed in the luggage bay.

She climbed onto the bus and took a seat by the window. This was her choice.

If this is what you want, why do you have to talk yourself into it?

* * *

"Beckett." Jack Turner stood in front of the table where Matt sat.

"Turner."

He took a bite of the sausage and egg sandwich that may as well have been rubber as far as he was concerned.

"What are you doing here?"

Matt frowned at the man. "Where else would I be?"

Turner ran a hand over his bald head. "Uh—"

"Why don't you sit?"

Turner dropped into the chair, and Matt focused on choking down his breakfast, though he sensed the man staring at him.

"You okay?"

"I'm fine."

His heart was on a bus headed to Portsville, but he wasn't the first person who had to live with heartbreak, and he wouldn't be the last. He crumpled the clear wrapper and gave the man his full attention.

"Where were you expecting me to be?"

Turner studied him, while Matt remained impassive under the man's scrutiny.

"Shouldn't you be at Sapphire Beach helping to set everything up?"

Matt quirked a brow. "Weren't you getting people to take care of that?"

"I'm not your enemy, Matt."

He sighed. Could the man have picked a worse time to have this conversation?

"Morningside is more than the place you work," Turner continued. "It's a community. You'll get the best experience if you participate in other activities and not simply focus on your patients."

"What do you want from me?" Matt glowered at the man. "I did what you asked me to do—spent hours planning your fundraiser.

"I spent my off-shift time decorating a stupid Christmas tree because the hospital was too cheap to ante up the money for a DJ. I traipsed all over town, begging people to contribute their products, doing things so far out of my comfort zone, I no longer recognize myself."

It had been the worst time of his life and the best. Matt stood. "My shift's over, and I'm leaving. If this means you don't renew my contract, so be it."

Despite his words in the cafeteria, he ended up at Sapphire Beach. Turner must have gotten people to help. Everything was the way Sunshine had envisioned it and described it to him.

Kenneth had set up his system at the far end of the beach, and music pulsed in the air. There were several long tables for the Blend-off Competition and a small stage.

He tucked his hands into his pocket. It was warmer than it had been the previous day. God had granted them the perfect weather to raise money for a worthy cause.

Already, several people, mostly children, were in the water, but their shrieks of happiness made him certain the fundraiser would be a success.

He snapped several photos and sent them to Sunshine. He

added a single line of text.

Wish you were here.

What was he doing? Hadn't he promised himself he wouldn't make her feel guilty for leaving? He turned and bumped into Ian.

"What are you doing here?"

Ian raised a brow and held up a ticket. "Why are *you* here?"

Matt growled. Why did everyone expect him to be somewhere else? "Where else would I be?"

"At the bus terminal with Sunshine."

"She didn't want me there."

"She didn't want any of us there. She snuck out of the house before anyone was awake." Ian met his gaze. "What are you doing, Matt? A fool could see that you're in love with her."

"What am I supposed to do? She made it clear she wanted to return to Portsville. What kind of man would I be if I forced her to choose between me and her career?"

Ian poked him in the chest. "What kind of man will you become if you don't offer her a choice?" Ian stalked away.

Was his friend right? Had letting Sunshine go been the wrong thing?

You young people complicate everything. Love is the most natural thing in the world. If you love the girl and she loves you back, you ask her to be your wife. Then you get married and start your life together.

Was his grandfather right? Was Ian? He had never met a woman like Sunshine. One who challenged him to see things another way and made him want to be better. In two weeks, she'd shaken up his world. For the better. Even his grandfather had been a beneficiary of the Sunshine Effect.

He was an idiot.

How was he going to survive the rest of his life without Sunshine when he couldn't go a day without her?

He should have followed her to Portsville and gotten a job in a hospital there. He would work as a janitor if he got to spend at least part of his week with her.

Matt checked his watch. Sunshine's bus had left twenty minutes ago. If he left now, he'd get to the next terminal before her. Then, either he would convince her to come home with him, or he'd follow her to Portsville.

Twenty

Epiphanies and Christmas Kisses

Sunshine glared at the couple across from her. They should get a hold of themselves. Their affection for each other was disgusting. *They* were disgusting.

Since the minute they'd sat, they'd gone into full Public Display Mode. Either he was playing with her hair or she was laying her head on his shoulder. Or they were stealing kisses as if they weren't aware everyone could see them.

"Aren't they cute?" The woman in the seat behind her leaned forward to whisper in her ear.

No, they weren't cute. They needed to slide a few inches apart so she wouldn't spend the next three hours mourning what she'd left behind.

"My husband and I met in college." The woman wiggled her ringed finger near Sunshine's ear. "Fifteen years and we're still in love."

She didn't want to hear it. Why was everyone rubbing their

togetherness bliss in her face?

A sound heart is the life of the flesh: but envy the rottenness of the bones.

What was she doing? Sunshine jerked her head to stare out at the passing scenery. Getting into a jealous rage because two college students dared to cuddle in her presence?

Was this her new normal? Would she get angry every time she was around a happy couple?

She worked as a florist for a wedding planner. How would she do her job effectively if she went into a blind rage every time she was around people in love?

I asked You for a sign, Lord, is this it? What does it mean?

An image of her sitting on her mother's veranda with Matt flashed in her mind.

I love everything about you. Sunshine, I love you. I'm so in love with you I don't know how I'm going to survive when you leave.

She was a fool. She'd had the opportunity of a lifetime—being loved by Matt—and she'd thrown it away. For what? A job? The chance to provide the backdrop for other people's happy endings while leaving hers behind?

"Stop the bus!" Sunshine jumped out of her seat, ignoring the passengers who stared at her as if she were mad, and stumbled toward the driver.

"Sir," she clung to the handrail behind the driver.

The man spared her one glance before returning his attention to the road.

"Miss, please take your seat."

"I can't. I need you to stop the bus." Her entire future hung in the balance and he wanted her to sit?

"Ma'am. This bus is on a schedule. The next stop will be at Cinnamon Hill in forty-five minutes. Please take your seat unless you want to be greeted by the police when we get there."

"Fine."

Sunshine's shoulders slumped as she trudged back to her seat. It would be a long trip.

* * *

Matt paced the length of the platform as he waited for Sunshine's bus to pull in. Either she would be happy to see him or horrified. His heart pounded until Matt had to remind himself it couldn't beat itself out of his chest.

God, I don't know if I'm doing the right thing. But love is too precious for me not to fight for it. Please let Sunshine be willing to take a chance on us.

A large coaster bus drove toward the terminal, and Matt swiped a hand down the leg of his pants. Was this the bus Sunshine was on?

His first instinct was to rush toward the doors as they opened. Only the surge of passengers prevented him from moving. The last thing he wanted to do was get pushed along with the crowd and end up stuck on the wrong bus.

She was the first person off the bus, quickly followed by a man in uniform. The driver? Matt squeezed forward. He only had a few minutes to plead his case.

"Sunshine."

Her head whipped toward him. "Matt."

He moved closer until he was mere inches away.

Her tongue darted out to wet her lips. "What are you doing here?"

"Funny thing about that, I realized I never asked you to stay. I need you to stay—" his voice broke, and he cleared his throat.

"What?" Her eyes searched his. "What are you saying, Matt?"

He was doing this all wrong. He stepped closer.

"I want you to stay in Orange Valley." He caressed the back of her hand. "I understand why you can't, so I'm moving to Portsville."

Her eyes widened. "You are? What about your job?"

He cupped her cheek. "I can be a doctor anywhere. I only have one chance to love you and be loved by you."

Except she'd never said she loved him. Matt became conscious of the passengers watching them, no longer interested in embarking or disembarking. The driver had stopped rooting around in the trunk and gaped at them.

"Sunshine—"

"I was on the way back to Orange Valley."

He blinked. "You were. Why?"

"I had an epiphany." She half-smiled. "I can be a florist anywhere. I only get one chance to love you and be loved by you."

A smile stole over his face. "You love me?"

"Uh-huh." She twined her arms around his neck. "Let me make it crystal clear. I'm so in love with you. I don't know how I'd live without you, and I refuse to try."

She pulled his head down to hers. "Now shut up and kiss me, Doctor Grump."

As his lips met hers, the cheers and whoops faded into the background.

Epilogue

One month later

Sunshine glanced at Matt. "I'll be another minute."

She added more sprigs of baby's breath and tied a bright blue ribbon around the bouquet, finishing it with a flourish.

After she'd resigned from the Bella Flora, she'd taken over the running of The Fair Child. Over the past few weeks, she'd expanded her offerings beyond the usual potted plants and cut flowers.

She and Jennifer Bell-McPherson from Belle's Garden had entered into a partnership. Jenny provided the flowers, and Sunshine did the floral arrangements for special occasions. They'd done a few weddings and engagement parties, but it was a start.

While she wasn't doing the level of floral design she'd done at Bella Flora, she also didn't have the same workload, leaving time for other things.

"Who's this for?" Matt tipped his chin toward the bouquet.

"Kyle. He's a first-time father who wanted to get something special for his wife. He's picking them up later today."

He twirled her ponytail around his hand. "So you're forcing me to end our lunch date early so you can come back to work?"

They were celebrating Shantoy's successful surgery. Morningside had donated money from the fundraiser to the teenager and three other patients.

She turned and wrapped her arms around his neck.

"Or," she kissed the side of his mouth. "We could take the bouquet with us and deliver it to him."

It was doable. She had Kyle's number. It would be simple enough to call.

He tugged her closer. "I like the way your brain works."

He captured her lips, and she sighed. She loved kissing Matt. She loved *him*. The bell over the door tinkled.

"Ugh."

The sound was both a blessing and a curse. She put some distance between her and Matt and adopted her most professional smile.

A couple dressed in T-shirts and jeans entered, both of them wearing dark wraparound glasses and ball caps tugged low on their heads.

"Hi, good afternoon. How may I help you?"

"Yes." The woman smiled. "We're looking for Sunshine?"

"You've found her."

The man nodded to Matt. "Is he an employee?"

Her cheeks warmed. "Uhm, no. Matt's my boyfriend."

She still couldn't believe she got to call him that.

"Okay." The man nodded. "Is it possible for you to close the shop for a few minutes? My fiancee and I would like to discuss business with you."

She tensed. Why would she need to close the shop for them to conduct business? Matt shifted closer to her.

"Please." The woman held out a hand.

Sunshine's gaze snagged on the diamond—while not huge, it was eye-catching. Surely people who could afford jewelry like that weren't there to rob them.

Lord? I could use a little help here.

She scanned the couple. The man was about her height, the woman a couple of inches shorter. Her instincts told her they weren't a threat.

She cleared her throat. "Matt, please close the door."

He growled, "Suppose they're ax murderers?"

Her lips twitched. "This is what I get for making you watch movies I consider classics." Trusting Matt to protect her, she turned her back to the couple.

"Matt, either we're going to trust God all the way or not trust Him at all."

Conscious of the couple listening to every word, she lowered her voice. "Do we aspire to be people who put their faith wholeheartedly in God? Or a couple who lives in fear?"

He scowled at the people behind her. "I want to be a couple who lives long enough to have that choice."

"Matt." She rested a hand on his arm.

"Fine." He jabbed his finger at the man. "Come with me."

Sunshine shook her head as the two men left to do a one-person job.

"Your boyfriend truly loves you." The woman's voice was sweet.

Sunshine grinned. "He does." She gestured to the men who were on their way back. "Sorry about the extra precaution, but it's not standard practice for me to lock the shop when doing business. I hope I didn't offend you."

Matt reclaimed his position beside her, his hand resting

against the small of her back.

The man took one of his fiancee's hands. "Are you sure you want to do this?"

The woman nodded.

"Even after that whole thing?" the man gestured to Sunshine and Matt.

The woman grinned. "Especially after that. Any couple who is that deliberate about pursuing God has my support."

"Okay." The man nodded and adopted a protective posture beside the woman that mirrored Matt's.

Sunshine frowned. Why would this couple act as if they needed protection from her and Matt?

The woman faced Sunshine. "I'd like you to do the flowers for my wedding."

She removed her shades, revealing brown eyes. Sunshine blinked. She looked familiar.

"In June." The woman continued as she removed her cap. Curly, dark-brown hair spilled over her shoulders. Sunshine gasped.

A tiny smile danced around the woman's mouth. "I tried to hire you before, but you quit and moved to another town."

Matt whispered in her ear. "Are they…?"

She nodded, unable to speak. Her gaze flicked to the man who'd also removed his shades and hat. Derek Walker and Nadia Barrett were in her shop.

Nadia Barrett and Derek Walker were in The Fair Child. In Orange Valley. Her eyes filled.

Nadia frowned. "Are you okay?"

She nodded.

Get it together, Sunshine.

At this rate, Derek and Nadia would retract their offer before she even had the chance to accept it. She gulped. "I'm fine. It's just that I—"

How much of her story should she share with this woman? A potential future client and the woman who'd catapulted to super-stardom in a brief time.

She's just a person.

Right.

"I wanted so badly to do your wedding flowers. I assumed it wouldn't happen after I left Bella Flora."

Nadia met her gaze. "I didn't want to work with Bella Flora. The only reason I hired them was to get to you."

Nadia clasped her hands together, and if Sunshine wasn't mistaken, there was a slight tremor.

"I'm a fan of your work and I'm determined to have you do my flowers. Can you add me to your schedule?" Nadia's eyes pleaded with her.

Why was she hesitating?

"Yes!"

Matt chuckled, and a huge grin spread over Nadia's face.

"Oh, good." Nadia sagged against Derek. "When Angela told me you'd returned home, I gave up on having you do my flowers. Then Angela said you were running your family's flower shop and suggested I call—"

"Angela did that?" Sunshine had assumed her former employer was angry that she'd resigned. She'd returned to Portsville after the holidays to clear up loose ends at the office and move out of her apartment.

"Yes." Nadia's smile was gentle. "She speaks highly of you. She asked me to tell you that if you ever tire of running this place, call her."

Tears pricked Sunshine's eyes. She hadn't expected this to

happen. God had gone before her and worked things out so she could be near her family and the man she loved without sacrificing her dreams.

"Thank you."

The words were both an acceptance of Nadia's offer and an acknowledgment of what God had done.

"Thank *you*." Nadia reached for her hand. "I'm eager to work with you. I promise I'm not a diva."

They exchanged numbers, and Derek and Nadia donned their disguises.

Derek dipped his chin. "Thanks for doing this." He grinned. "Now maybe we can talk about something other than wedding flowers."

Nadia tucked her arm around his. "Talk to you soon."

Sunshine restrained her excitement until the tinkle of the bell announced her guests' departure. She counted to fifteen in her head before whirling to Matt.

"Nadia Barrett wants me to do her wedding flowers." She squealed. "I'm doing the flowers for Nadia's and Derek's wedding."

"I heard." Matt rested his hands on her waist. "Do I need to become a superstar for you to be that enthusiastic about seeing me?"

"Aww." Sunshine slipped her arms around his neck. "Did I hurt Doctor Grump's feelings?"

"I'm a little concerned about how eager my girlfriend was to meet another man."

She sobered. "That was me fangirling. I know what's real."

This was real. The bond between her and Matt had deepened in the month they'd been dating. Enough that Sunshine already dreamed of them getting married.

For everything, there is a season.

"I love you, Matt." God had proven He would work things out in their proper time. She'd trust Him with her relationship with Matt.

She leaned in to kiss him. For now, she'd enjoy kissing her boyfriend, leaving the future in God's hands.

* * *

Join my email community to read the bonus epilogue of Matt and Sunshine's happy day! Sign up here: https://BookHip.com/DVRCZHC

* * *

Did you enjoy Matt and Sunshine's story? Please consider leaving a review. Thank you!

Author's Note

Thank you for reading Matt and Sunshine's story. I hope you enjoyed spending time with this couple as much as I did. This story almost didn't exist, but I'm so glad it does.

One thing on my author wishlist was contributing a story to an anthology. I love story collections and have discovered some of my favorite authors through reading anthologies.

In May 2023, I read an invitation to contribute to an anthology that fit into my writing schedule.

After some brainstorming, I had the perfect idea for my anthology story: I'd write a twin switch. I'd publish the first novella a month before the anthology, and the second story would be in the anthology.

Now you may wonder, what happened? Why is Sunshine *not* a twin?

After finishing both stories, I started worrying that the one I'd intended to submit for the anthology wasn't "Christmassy" enough.

When I shared my dilemma with my husband, his response was flippant, "Write a new story".

Dear reader, let me tell you, those words struck panic in my heart. Usually, I have several story ideas I want to write, but when he said those words, my mind went blank.

"I have nothing," I told him, "not a single idea".

"Well," he stroked his chin. "I may have an idea."

The essence of his idea was an atheist falling in love with a girl who loves Christmas. Since I'd wanted to write a grumpy-sunshine romance, the story of Matt and Sunshine was born.

I loved writing this story and watching Matt transform from the grumpy man who didn't believe in Christ to the man who surrendered to his Savior. Sunshine's journey to accept herself was also inspiring.

I hope both characters remind you that your worth is found in God. When we take our troubles to Him, even the ones that seem insignificant, He hears us.

God will, and does, answer our prayers. He may not answer in the way we want Him to, but it's always with our eternal salvation in mind.

If you enjoyed Sunshine and Matt's story, please consider leaving a review so that other readers can discover this novella.

About Aminata

Aminata Coote's love affair with books began with an upside-down copy of Silas Marner. She's passionate about helping women understand the truth of the Bible for themselves.

She writes stories and books that point to a God bigger than our failings and provide hope to others. Aminata is also the author of several Bible studies and devotionals.

She lives in Montego Bay, Jamaica with her husband and son.

Connect with her on her website, aminatacoote.com, or on Instagram or Facebook @aminatacoote. Learn more about her books at https://aminatacoote.com/books-by-aminata-coote/.

Sign up for Aminata's newsletter at https://tinyurl.com/FreeReadingJournal for a free reading journal.

Other Books by Aminata

Inspirational Contemporary Romance

Orange Valley Series
His Perfect Wife
His Perfect Match
His Perfect Family
His Perfect Choice

Christmas with the Porters
A Husband for Christmas
A Family for Christmas
A Wife For Christmas
A Daughter for Christmas

The Firefighters of Orange Valley
Falling For Her Fake Wedding Date
Falling For Her Student's Single Dad
Falling For Her Grumpy Neighbor

Sweet Haven

Her Rock Star Husband
The Mother of His Child
Her Best Friend's Secret

Christmas in Orange Valley
The Doctor's Christmas Miracle
The CEO's Christmas Surprise

Hearts Unveiled
Finding Peace in Orange Valley
Finding Love in Orange Valley
Finding Joy in Orange Valley

Orange Valley Shorts
How It Began: His Perfect Wife Prequel
I'll Wait For You: His Perfect Family Prequel

Devotionals
How To Find Your Gratitude Attitude
Draw Closer 52-Week Devotional Journal
Praying Your Way Through Social Media: Reflections for
Christian Artists and Entrepreneurs (collaboration with
Latasha Strachan)
God Sees You: 21 Devotions for the Woman Who Feels
Invisible
The Battle Is Not Yours: 21 Devotions for Spiritual Warfare
God Is In Control: 21 Devotions on God's Sovereignty

Learn more about my books at
https://tinyurl.com/ACooteBooks

Newsletter Sign-up

Join Aminata's newsletter community and get a bonus epilogue of Sunshine and Matt's wedding day. Sign up here: https://BookHip.com/DVRCZHC.

Join Aminata's community

Website: https://aminatacoote.com

Facebook: https://www.facebook.com/AminataCoote

Instagram: https://www.instagram.com/aminatacoote/

* * *

Book Club Guide

If you'd like to read *The Doctor's Christmas Miracle* with your club, check out the book club guide that's available on my website for free.